THE SONG OF THE SLEEPERS
*A NOVELLA*

# THE CHILD OF THE GREENWOOD

## JOSHUA WALKER

*Praise for The Child of the Greenwood & The Song of the Sleepers*

The Child of the Greenwood *is very much a small peek into what is evidently a huge saga, and the sheer scale of this series is hinted at on every page. This was a wonderful story from an exciting new voice in epic fantasy!*

**LL MacRae, Author of** *The Iron Crown*

*Soul-crunching moments of darkness and despair mixed with a hijinx-filled quest storyline with three loveable characters. There's something about the Nestlers and Burrowers that warms your heart, even when a few pages later, Walker might devastate you with unexpected heartbreak. With prose and characters this good, you'll wish there were 600 more pages!*

**Dave Lawson, Author of** *The Envoys of War*

*A captivating story of courage and resilience, set in a beautiful world that is brilliantly realized ... Walker has given us an appetizer that leaves you begging for dinner.*

**Scott Palmer, Author of** *A Memory of Song*

*The raw emotion I felt pouring off the pages is unparalleled with any other book I have read.*

**Kristen Shafer,** *SFF Insiders*

*A powerful, beautiful story about loss and how we deal with it.*

**Nicholas W Fuller, Booktube**

*Both timelines weave together seamlessly, as one posits questions the other answer ... to demonstrate that Q'ara is large, living world full of magic and mystery.*

**Livia J Elliot, Author of** *The Genesis of Change*

*So much happens in this novella. Loss, grief, coming to terms with the harsh truths of life and death and betrayal. It's manoeuvred expertly by Joshua, who once again works wonders with his storytelling.*

**Noah Isaacs, Author of** *Memories of Tomorrow*

*The ability to craft a tone for not only the settings but the characters throughout, is masterful. The prose is rich, tactile, and effortless to read.*

**Vivian, Goodreads Reviewer**

*Blending the past and present in a seamless narrative, this story keeps you on the edge of your seat, offering thrilling twists and captivating moments at every turn.*

**Carina, Goodreads Reviewer**

## BY JOSHUA WALKER

**The Song of the Sleepers**

0.5) The Rest to the Gods
1) An Exile of Water & Gold
1.5) The Child of the Greenwood
2) An Empire of Dirt & Lies *(Forthcoming)*
2.5) The Celestial Tears of Dying Light *(Forthcoming)*

Copyright © 2024 by Joshua Walker

First published in 2025 by Joshua Walker.

This edition published in 2025 by Joshua Walker.

No part of this publication may be reproduced, distributed, or transmitted in any form or by any means, including photocopying, recording, or other electronic or mechanical methods, without the prior written permission of the publisher, except as permitted by Australian copyright law. For permission requests, contact the author.

The moral right of the author has been asserted. All rights reserved.

The story, all names, characters, and incidents portrayed in this production are fictitious. No identification with actual persons (living or deceased), places, buildings, and products is intended or should be inferred.

No AI was used in the production of this publication, including any interior or exterior artwork. No part of this publication may be used to further any algorithm or learning techniques of any AI-based programs.

Edited by Sarah Chorn, https://sarahchornedits.com.

Proofread by Isabelle Wagner, https://theshaggyshepherd.wordpress.com.

Cover art and design by Stefanie Saw, https://www.seventhstarart.com.

Map design by Joshua Hoskins, Noctua Cartography (@Noctua_Maps).

Chapter Headings by Joshua Walker.

ISBN 978-0-6486427-7-0 (paperback)

ISBN 978-0-6486427-8-7 (hardback)

ISBN 978-0-6486427-6-3 (ebook)

*To those who are alone,*
*May you find comfort, reassurance, and kinship in Jilo's story.*
*May the light go with you.*

# Contents

1. NOW — 2
2. THEN — 14
3. NOW — 24
4. THEN — 35
5. NOW — 44
6. THEN — 55
7. NOW — 65
8. THEN — 76
9. NOW — 86
10. THEN — 96
11. NOW — 114
ABOUT THE AUTHOR — 126

## A note on the English language

Dear reader,

Before we begin, I thought I should let you know that I am unabashedly Australian, and a result you might find some spellings in this book that you do not agree with.

Firstly, our main character, Jilo, is an unexpected **traveller**, and because of this, he hasn't packed **pyjamas** for the journey. They are after all, clothes that are designed to keep one **cosy,** a feeling which Jilo certainly does not have much experience with.

Additionally, you may see buildings with several **storeys,** fire that **smoulders**, and **sceptics** aplenty. After all, my characters are often in **dialogue** with the kind of folk who are (frustratingly) morally **grey.**

I promise, I'm not an **arsehole,** but I won't **apologise** for writing in British English. It is after all the superior form, my **defence** of which is totally justified.

Josh

Sethi Ranges
Ghabbat
Lake Sethiliquin
Ghabat River
The Rocklands
Piat
Tel-Kathan
The Hidden Forest
Providence
Aobia
River Tornet
The Heart
The Viaduct

# The Continent of Q'ara

- Port Town
- The Heartstring
- Adira River
- The Outfields
- Adira
- Relond
- To Na'ar

*"It's so much darker when a light goes out than it would have been if it had never shone."*

– John Steinbeck, The Winter of Our Discontent

# NOW

## *2055 AS*

L**YN-CHEE.** *THE LINGERING DEATH.* It began with blades under the fingernails and concluded with a thousand precise cuts across the body.

Jilo should have suspected he would succumb to this: a method of torture that originated with his own people, the extinct tribe of Sai-Kathan. The irony of his suffering was not lost on Jilo. It was like having his forgotten heritage remembered for a fleeting moment, only to have a part of it thrown back in his face.

He steeled himself and closed his mind to pain, like he had every day since he'd learned to walk. Whether through lessons learned from his parents and the clan leaders of Sai-Kathan or the precise survivalism of the Hidden Ones taught to him many years later, Jilo knew well the ways to seal the faucet from which pain and fear flowed.

He controlled his expression and bit back his tears as they filled his eyes. His body was betraying him. He was fixed in a chair, his head bowed down and clamped in place between two rods of timber. The only thing he could see was the careful extraction of his fingernail on his right pinkie. The stream of blood that welled beneath the nail was constant and flowed as freely as a river, dripping onto the tiled ground.

"All you need to do is tell us the truth and we'll let you go," crooned his torturer, a Piatic nobleman named Ardyr. "We want you to tell us how you came to know about the grindel and what it does to ... people like you."

"I've told you," Jilo managed to spit between heaving breaths, "it isn't called that." The blood was nearly hypnotic to look at as it landed on the floor. *Drip, drip, drip.*

"I don't care what you call it. It isn't yours to take." *Drip.*

"It belonged to my people. It is a source of great tradition and pride." Anger flushed Jilo's face, but he bit his tongue. *If I speak out of turn, I'll bleed even more,* he thought.

"It has been in our possession for years, Kathani." Jilo felt Ardyr's gaze upon him. "When the Theradoran Empire first took it, they saw what the grindel could do to rats. They gave it to us to try on your furry friends. I can get the permission I need from the priests to use it on you too. So tell me the truth or I'll keep plucking you like a chicken." The Piatic man seized Jilo's hand once more, and he felt the cold of metal claws press down on his next fingernail. "Let's try something else, Jilo of the Sai-Kathan people. How can a man who looks so young be older than my father? How can you appear ageless, and yet you are also in your eighth decade? Surely, it has something to do with the grindel."

Jilo sucked in another breath. He could do this. He could put away the pain, force it into a place he would not dare go until he was ready to face it. But he *was* exhausted. "I don't know. Perhaps it *is* something to do with the spear. But I don't know. That is the truth."

The pool of blood at his feet was now large enough that he could see his weary face reflected back at him. Blackened eyes, greasy long hair hanging in strands about his head. His study was not long-lived, however, as a familiar, heavy object was thrown into the puddle, splashing red up his legs. The thing that they called grindel, his father's glowing spear. Ka-Del, meaning *Spear of Life*, as Ne-Lo the Visionary had named it when he'd created the blade. It lay in his blood, a strong blue aura about it, signifying danger.

Jilo stifled a sob at the sight of it, but he stopped it before the tears could fall. He was surprised at the heartache of seeing Ka-Del here after all this time. Ka-Del had been the heartbeat of his people and his family. "Please," Jilo begged. "Take what you want. Take my life if you must, but don't allow my spilled blood to stain this spear."

He felt the timber clamp around his head release moments later, the tension expiring like the dying rumble of a storm. Ardyr grabbed a fistful of Jilo's long, black hair, shoving his neck backwards. After having been held in place for such a long time, it cracked from the sudden movement.

"Fine," was all the Piatic man said before he shoved Jilo violently. The collision sent Jilo and the chair flying backwards across the stone-floored chamber. Ardyr screamed in rage, seizing Jilo's hair again as he rammed the chair across the floor, letting go as it crashed into the wall behind them. Jilo's head swung like a doll's and hit the wall. A formidable darkness stole his consciousness away in the blink of an eye ...

When Jilo awoke later that night, he winced at the dull pain that flared across the back of his skull. He was finally alone. His hand was still locked against the armrest beside him, but the bleeding had stopped.

Keys jingled in the basement door, coming from the other side. *Perfect timing,* he grimaced.

"Are you there, Cousin?" came a small voice. A smile danced across Jilo's face. It could not be ...

The small, weasel-like creature who had called him cousin waltzed into the basement room as though it was as familiar as his home. Clev was a Nestler of the Hidden Ones, the folk that Jilo had known for well over sixty years. Clev had been an elder of the Hidden Forest for all that time, and though he was old now, he still had a spring in his step. His equally spritely nephew, Scov, was also with him, wedging the basement door open.

"Cousins," Jilo croaked in greeting. He nodded at his arms, which had since been re-bound in front of him. "Get me out of these?"

"Scov! A blade, perchance?" Clev asked, stepping up to look at Jilo's bandaged hand, dark brown with the stains of dried blood. "Good Earth, what have they done to you? Your fingers—"

"Yes," Jilo murmured. "They've seen better days. I'm not sure I can be of much use."

"So Clev and Scov will just leave you here?" Clev scoffed.

Jilo smirked. He'd lived with the Hidden Ones for longer than he'd lived with humans, at this point. They'd helped him find his way and, now, find Ka-Del again. But he could never adjust to how they all referred to themselves in the third person. "We'll need to be quick getting out of here. I can't fight with my hands and I'm not much of a kicker."

"If you can climb a damn tree, you can kick, Jilo," said Scov with an edge to his voice. "Now we escape this Piatic hellhole."

Scov whipped out a thin blade, curved and sharp enough to catch a glint of moonlight on its edge. An Izog was a Hidden One's weapon of choice, Nestler and Burrower alike. The small blades could pare limbs from bones quicker than one could ever see, and Jilo had used them as a younger man to skin game. They were no bigger than a human-sized hunting dagger.

"Keep your hands tight, Cousin Jilo," Scov said, centring the blade on the ropes that bound Jilo's bandaged and bloody hands. One swift motion later, Scov had cut right through them, leaving

Jilo a free man. Both Nestlers cut the ropes around his waist too and searched the room for an exit.

"La!" Jilo swore in Kathani. There was nothing here that would allow them to escape besides the door the Nestlers had entered from.

Clev peered at him. "We're thinking the same thing, aren't we?" He smoothed his whiskers as he waited for Jilo to fill the silence.

Jilo gulped. "We're going to have to fight our way through. Do either of you know where Ka-Del is now?"

Clev and Scov looked at one another, horrified. "You mean to tell us that Ka-Del is still with them? We thought you had gotten it already!"

"I had." Jilo grimaced. "But when they found me, they took Ka-Del again. They wanted to know about Ka-Del's capabilities, but I gave them nothing."

"The Empire has had that spear for years, Cousin." Scov frowned. "It is impossible that they would not have discovered its capabilities themselves."

"I'm not so sure the Empire divulges the scope of its knowledge, even to allies like Piat. They beat me after they realised *lyn-chee* was not doing what they expected. I think the spear strengthened me, somehow." He recalled the blue aura around the spear as it had lain in a pool of his blood, a colour he'd seen often in his past. "I passed out and woke up to you two arriving."

"Well," Clev said. "We must find Ka-Del, Jilo. We have no other option. It cannot stay here; it's too powerful. Us Nestlers know what it's like when humans take in artefacts of great power."

"May the Good Earth protect us," Scov said as he ran up the short set of steps that led from the doorway into the chamber. "Step quietly, Cousin Jilo, and maybe we will make it out of here alive."

Jilo let the others through the doorway, slowly swinging it closed behind him so it would not squeak.

"Do you know the way, Cousin?" Clev whispered, his snout so shiny in the dark hallway Jilo could barely make out his features. "Ka-Del could be anywhere in this place."

Jilo shook his head. "I don't even know where we are, Clev."

"Governor's office, on South-East Street," Scov said. "The building shares a small annex with the city's penitentiary."

"That was where we were going to go if you were not here, Jilo," explained Clev.

"I doubt I was supposed to live through this ordeal," Jilo said. "But I am in your navigational hands, Cousins. And, um—" He looked down at his own messily bandaged hands. "No pun intended."

Clev snorted as Scov suppressed a chuckle. "The guards here are slack, and the Empire's priests don't seem to be around. Keep your movements quiet and your head low, and they'll be none the wiser. Many of them should've been making the rounds tonight, but, as we discovered, there is a side room with a great wooden door closing it off, and it is filled with whiskey and dice."

"Do you think they would keep Ka-Del in there?" Scov asked as they began to move up the stairwell.

"No," Jilo said. "Ardyr wanted it for his father, the governor, to give back to Therador. His brother, Royg, said as much when they brought me in. They had it under contract, but for what, I never found out."

"How many of these Luminous items does Therador have in their grasp?" Scov asked. "They want to use the collective force of them against us all, Scov fears."

Jilo nodded. "If we do not reclaim Ka-Del, I fear the tides of war will turn."

"Then we can't give them that chance, Cousin," Scov said, an edge to his voice.

Clev nodded as they came to a hallway that ran adjacent to the top of the stairs. "Our forces already struggle in the Adiran Outfields, and now they march to the Mountain Pass. This will be the final knife in the back of the alliance. Jurin and his priests will take whatever they can get, short of securing the full breadth of Luminosity from the Aobians."

The image of the Theradoran heir and his cronies, Priests of Dirt, still sent shivers down Jilo's spine years after his first encounter with them. The kind of ruthless, insane, and overzealous tyrants that would watch the world burn before realising they would succumb to the same flames. Therador was a barbaric place, thanks to the priests and their twisted perception of human purpose. People in Therador worked until their hands bled, until their minds were lost, until they collapsed, thirsty and overburdened. If they did not, they were fed back into the earth—alive—an exchange with the land for their poor ethic. If you did not make yourself forever useful, you did not deserve life.

The walls in the governor's office were adorned with sconces of small flames, a low-lying glow lighting their way through the building. The rooms here lacked doors, so Jilo knew that any chance of finding Ka-Del would mean risking their lives to investigate.

But he knew what his father's staff looked like, sounded like. He knew the subtle coloured glows it gave off, symptoms of its creation. It had been assembled centuries ago from the wood of giant, dying trees. He knew the hiss that emanated from it when someone Ka-Del did not like got close. The spear had never been like that with him though. Even after his father—

"Cousin," Clev said, shoving Jilo back into a crevice in the wall. "Stay in the darkness. Trouble awaits."

A silhouette of crooked horns, like branches, danced on the walls of the hallway before them. The outline of the figure's body was crude and haunting. Behind them, the quiet clinking of a chain rang, attached via the shadow to the outline of another creature the size of a dog.

"Priests of Dirt," whispered Scov, shivering. "Why are they here?"

Jilo pursed his lips. "Ka-Del. This is worse than we thought. They're desperate for it. If Piat can't return it safely to them, they'll come for it themselves."

"Go back to the stairwell," Clev whispered. "Don't let them see you, Cousin."

"What about—" Jilo began, but Clev smothered his mouth with a furry paw, sharp nails scratching his cheeks.

"Go! Back to the basement. They have hounds to sniff out you *and* Ka-Del. Whichever is worse, we'll never know if you stay here."

"I'll be cornered!" Jilo fought off Clev's paw. The hound's shadow at the end of the long hall whipped its head in their direction.

"Leave it to us, Cousin."

With a hefty kick, Clev planted both feet into Jilo's chest, sending him back towards the stairs. Scov leapt down the hallway as Jilo's sight darkened and he fell backwards, down each step with a hard bounce until he landed before the roughshod, wooden door that he'd been sealed behind moments prior.

He respected Clev. He and Scov were like family to Jilo, and the respect they shared was not to be tampered with. But this was not right. He would not stand by and watch the two Nestlers get hurt, or worse, in their attempt to defend him and his father's spear.

He groaned as the halls filled with the ring of steel, curses, and crashes that he had hoped they would not ignite on this eve.

A blood-curdling scream was the first thing he was met with once he reached the hallway again. He squinted as he ran, weaponless, *handless,* towards the enemy and the leaping shadows of the two Nestlers. One was hooked around the throat of a priest while the other was fending off a barking-mad hound with a knife. The intersecting hall was now adorned with lamplight, confusing Jilo even more as he skidded to a stop in front of an unsuspecting man. Ardyr, the pathetic nobleman who had taken his fingernails from him. Without hesitation, Jilo swept his leg up, right into the man's crotch. Funnily enough, it felt like there wasn't much there, but Ardyr went head over heels, down to the ground, grasping at his manhood.

"Felt like I was kicking a woman," Jilo breathed. "Never had it cut off, have you?"

He leapt over the cursing man, towards another set of stairs that lead to the next floor of the governor's office. Priests of Dirt fought with a tangle of Piatic guards against the two Nestlers, who, combined, reached no higher than Jilo's stomach. But they would not be put down. The mettle of the Hidden Ones was not to be tested, as Jilo had made the mistake of thinking many times before. At the top of the stairs, one priest was swinging a hefty iron bar with both hands, desperately trying to push the Nestlers back. Clev and Scov were surrounded, pushed closer to the stairs by some of their assailants and pushed back by the priest who waited right above Jilo.

There was no time to wait. He sucked in a breath.

This was going to hurt.

Running towards the stairs, he gripped the rails with both hands as hard as he could, screaming out in pain and alerting the priest, who whirled around to see him. As the priest lost his footing and fell, Scov's tiny body could be seen holding onto their robes. Jilo's momentum allowed him to thrust his knee forward, smacking the priest right in the skull-masked face. The priest's head knocked against the stone wall after it ricocheted off Jilo's knee, and his body went still. Scov immediately jumped up, patting himself down as though his fur was unkempt.

"Scov!" Jilo cried, looking up. "Look! It's Clev!"

The older Nestler was fending off a hound, two priests, and a hefty swathe of Piatic guardsmen as he edged the top of the staircase, stuck in the same place as the felled priest before him.

Jilo's breath caught as Scov screamed, "NO!" and the suddenly fragile body of Clev was scooped up by a huge hound's jaw.

"Nephew!" Clev gasped, trying to reach out an arm as the hound snatched him away from the stairs.

Teeth gnawed through skin, bone, and cartilage, the grating sound filling Jilo's head. Blood streamed over the hound's black lips as Clev let out something akin to a quick and sharp sigh. He was so suddenly, pitifully, dead.

# THEN

## *1887 AS*

THE LAST DAYS OF summer stole what was left of the boy's soul. The hot afternoon air contrasted the frigid mornings when the tents were overlaid with icy dew. The sun sang life for those below, but it recoiled quickly at the sign of the moon.

The dead stuff on the ground was thick and unctuous, a result of coagulating blood, sticky and tar-like in the midday warmth. But at night, the parts loosened, a mere imitation of what the dead had once been, barely reanimated. At night, they were more like soup than bodies.

"Remember, son, what we have been given. It is our privilege to tend this land, to respect the gift we have been given here on Q'ara. The earth is constantly changing. It will adapt to the existence of life as surely as the sun will set and the moon will rise." Jilo's father mostly taught him the same principles on repeat, though Jilo knew he meant well. Look after the earth, respect your elders, and *never* tread outside the borders of Kathani land.

Three days ago, life had changed for Kathan forever, and now, the borders were more rigid than they'd ever been. The mysterious sickness that lay in the waters of the River Tomei had taken a turn for the worse after months of predictions from the Sha'men that had led nowhere: that it was a sign of the old gods or a cleansing spirit of the earth in the water. But as Jilo saw it, it was much simpler than that. Something had infected the water, and now, anyone or anything who drank from it died, melting from the inside out.

Now, as Jilo walked the dirty pathways that strung his people's tents together, the Sai-Kathan tribe, he knew this would really be the end of the Kathani as they knew it. A once-nomadic people, the Kathani had come to Q'ara by way of conquering their greatest fear: subservience to the tyranny of another human faction on their original homeland. Now, more than three millennia later, the Kathani were local to the wildland that bridged Aobia and beyond to the deserts of the south. Here, they cared for the animals of the earth and the trees and other flora in the ways they had always wanted to, before they'd had to flee their original home. Where that was, nobody seemed to know anymore.

The wildland was a mixture of drenched, humid rainforest and the desert terrain of the south. More than that, it was home.

But not for long.

"Come, Jilo," came the rumbling voice of his father, a brute of a man and the tribe-father of Sai-Kathan itself. Hiro Sai-Laia stared at the mess of melting bodies strewn across the ground of Sai-Kathan's tracks. In his hand he carried Ka-Del, the heirloom of every Sai-Kathan leader, which was glowing a deep and dark blue. The blue was so strong in its tone that it seemed to creep up his father's arm to the elbow. "Keep your boots rolled up over your knees. This Sickness is no ordinary poison. I fear the worst for our people and this place." His deep voice broke, a sound Jilo had never thought he'd hear. "This beautiful, beautiful place."

Three days and it had already come to this? His father had already sent runners to Tel-Kathan, the tree tribe, and Rei-Kathan, the lake tribe, both in the northern parts of the wildland, to warn them of what would come. The moonlight had started to soak the forest floor now, and in the distance, comforting flickers of natural light from the mushrooms lit the way through the camp. Would they really have to leave? And if they did, would that not simply delay the inevitable? It was only a matter of time until the Sickness would reach the other tribes. Then what? Aobia? Or north, to the lands the barbarians of Therador settled a thousand years after the Kathani people?

"Where will we go, Father?" Jilo asked.

"Tel-Kathan," Hiro replied simply, like it was no great toll. Owls chirped to one another in the trees while the breeze rustled the canopies. The sounds of the dying, on the other hand, were quiet. A silent poison. Yesterday, when the Sai leaders had convened to discuss their plan, Jilo had helped his mother, Talei, tend the sick. They'd worn tan gloves, and cut-outs over their mouths, so as to prevent more contact than needed.

# THE CHILD OF THE GREENWOOD

Jilo had watched a baby melt, its insides falling into the arms of its mother. By the time they had dug a hole, the once-child had been nothing but a composite of parts, broken down into a kind of stew. Jilo had left, then, escaping into the forest. He'd run, enough that he hadn't been able to hear his mother warning people not to step in the covered-up hole.

That had been just over twenty-four hours ago. Now, they had already grown accustomed to getting their shoes stuck in the stringy mess of melted bodies. Walking through them reminded Jilo of biting into a melted cheese and cabbage flatbread, the ooze of the cheese contrasting with the sour crunch of the fermented cabbage. The thought made his stomach curdle for the first time in a few hours, and he leant over a bush to let loose burning vomit.

"Boy," Hiro said. "Do not think on it. Whatever food or drink you have left in you, keep it. I do not know when we will drink clean water next."

They were parched, both him and his father. The tribe-leaders had tested the river water with several unlucky volunteers, and so far, nothing short of thrice boiling it seemed to work. But drinking it was like drinking iron, let alone waiting for the stuff to cool in the thick summer heat. Now, here they were, searching the forest for red lotus ponds that they could draw both food and drink from alike.

"Will the pond water be clean, Father?" Jilo asked through gritted teeth, the burn of vomit dancing upon his gums.

His father shrugged. "It's mosquito season, Son. I would never look to a pond to harvest anything but the lotus flowers, but this is an unprecedented crisis. We need water, Jilo. Let us take what we can, boil the stuff, and be done with it. Hopefully there are enough freshwater ponds across the forest to keep us satiated until we reach Tel-Kathan."

On their backs, Jilo and his father wore huge skins, wax-sealed and roughly the size of a bedroll. They could each carry a few gallons, and despite his age, Jilo was the strongest fourteen-year-old in the tribe. His father could've found no better person for the job.

Their trek had sent them into the dark heart of the rainforest. Between the trees were voids of black, unless the odd purple glow of the mushrooms and streams were present. The best thing they had with them otherwise was Ka-Del, which offered just enough light to navigate the bleak brush. Jilo and his father did not hesitate to make a sound as they moved; vibrations in the forest floor would keep the spiders in their hidden alcoves, the tree-snakes in their branches.

Red lotus was abundant in the area, and they quickly came across a sizeable pond, the second one of the evening. Again, it was filthy, and Hiro shook his head, muttering.

"Surely, we can take it and clean it?" Jilo asked.

"No," his father murmured in reply. "The muck alone will sicken us. We need a cleaner pond." He breathed deeply as though calming himself, but Jilo already knew what was coming. His father's anger was a force to be reckoned with, a surge the size of a storm. "Sai-La!" Hiro swore, planting Ka-Del's spearhead into the earth.

*Curse the river.* Jilo translated the words in his mind. Their tribe, the Sai-Kathan, were the river-dwellers. This was their home, their life. Yet now the very thing they depended upon offered up nothing more than death.

"Father," Jilo said in a low tone, watching his father kneeling in the mud, breathing heavily. "We can find another. There are ponds everywhere out here. We just need time—"

"There is no time! Useless child!" Hiro roared, standing and shoving Jilo with both palms, sending him skidding across the muddy ground that surrounded the reedy pond.

Jilo tasted dirt and felt the sting of it graze his cheek as his body came to a stop. "I'm sorry, Father, I—"

"You're good for nothing, boy," Hiro heaved. "I brought you to carry water, and *only* carry it. I did not bring you to speak daft words and fill me with false hopes. *Be aware that idols are always hidden in those you love.* Ne-lo, from the Founding Verses." He spat the words like venom off the fangs of a snake. He always used the Founding Verses, the original words of wisdom of the Kathani, to bully Jilo into what he wanted. Jilo knew he was not enough in his father's eyes. Even after all they'd been through the last couple days, he knew he would never be fit to lead these people. Jilo glanced at his father and saw a lone tear trailing down his cheek. His father never cried.

"Now, we go back," Hiro said, hulking away and wiping spit from his wiry beard with the cuff of his gloves. "I will not lose my way in this forest tonight. Not when I am needed the most. Tomorrow, we try once more before we set out with whoever we have left."

*I will not lose my way tonight.* Jilo got up and stumbled through the mud in his father's footsteps. He smirked. It was never 'we'. There was no 'we'. Even with his mother around, he knew his father's hubris was unbreakable, and insufferable for everybody else. Still, they clung to him. For all his shortcomings, Hiro was a good leader. He was the hundredth in his line. He knew his duty, and it filled his life, more than his own wants, more than the needs of his family.

As they walked back through the winding pathways of luminescent flora, Jilo squinted to see his father's outline in the growing dark as he ruminated. He would never be like Hiro. He would never put the needs of his work above the needs of the people who loved him, who depended on him. He would never treat his children like inconveniences.

They continued in silence as Jilo made these same resolutions again and again, the way he did whenever his father's temper began to break like a storm. They were hopeless resolutions, but he needed them. He needed their fantasy. He knew the life he led was only going in one direction: to lead the Sai-Kathan once his father became a tribe elder. He was being moulded into someone else's shape. He'd never asked for that.

Trees became a monotonous blur as they stepped through the rainforest, the silence of it staggering Jilo as it always did. The careful terrain and assortment of harmonious life were nothing to bat an eye at. Despite his feelings about his destiny, Jilo knew this place would always be home. No matter what happened.

As the moonlight opened up through the trees and the hint of firelight from the tribe came back into view, the perfect silence finally broke. At first, it was like a rising swell, like water being poured into a pot from another vessel, starting slowly and building to a crescendo of swirls and spatters. Hiro tucked himself behind a line of bamboo, listening intently. Jilo came to his side and said nothing.

"Do you hear that, boy?" his father whispered over the rushing sound. Ka-Del was a grim, violent blue now, its glow competing for the light the moon offered.

"It sounds like water, Father."

Hiro looked into his son's eyes with an intensity that could rival the brightest flame. "Whatever I say, you do. Am I understood?"

"Yes, Father."

"Stay close. I fear the worst." He sniffed. Hiro was crying … again? Like he knew something was about to go very, *very* wrong.

Pulling out from behind the curtain of bamboo, Jilo stepped in every place his father's feet went, darting through the thickets of forestry. The sound was loud now, filling his ears entirely, save for one other sound: screams.

"No!" Hiro cried as they ran. "No! Talei, my love!"

*Mama!* Jilo suppressed the panic he felt. He would best his father at this one day. He would not let his feelings dominate his actions. Quickly, however, he realised that that was impossible.

As they ran towards their tribe, the River Tomei lifted as menacingly high as ocean waves in a storm, crashing about as though it were alive. And it was. This Sickness was not just a poison. It was a parasite. Jilo watched in horror as the water climbed as high as the zhate trees and the great pan-din palms. The water crashed down and caused the rest of the river to stretch and expand, like a rug being flung out in front of one's hands. The uncontained water quickly began to pool across the dead bodies of the Sai-Kathan, filling tents and knocking over lanterns and torches.

The natural lights of the mushrooms and loi-reeds extinguished the second the water touched them, and the people of Sai-Kathan ran like beasts, crying for help. As the water leapt and soared, it continued to swell more, growing to a thirty-foot-high wall.

Jilo ran in the direction of their home, the hall of the tribe-leader. Mother would be there, tending the sick, exhausted, and thirsty. And if he did not get there in time, she would not make it out. This water that had once fed them and given them life now stood as tall as the tsunami waves in the stories of old, an apex predator over all living things.

Hiro had already run off, bundling people into groups and sending them back into the trees that he and Jilo had just emerged from. "Run, and do not look back!" Jilo heard him say.

"Father, we must find Mother!" Jilo yelled over the calamity of noise.

Tears streaked down his father's face. His long, black hair was in shambles, and his eyes were gaunt and black. Shivers ran down Jilo's spine. "No, Father. I will not listen to you say—"

Hiro reached out and grabbed Jilo by the wrists. "There is no time, boy. I know my duty. It is with my people. Do you know yours? If you do not save her, you yourself will not survive the next time we meet."

Hiro ... He was going to abandon his wife for the people? Jilo held back another sick retch as he panted in disbelief. His father shoved him away, sending him spinning.

"Go! Find your mother, boy. Do what it is that you should do."

That was when the wall came down, the water grinning at them as it fell, an ugly consumer. The flood began, and Jilo could do nothing but stand there, hopeless, and hold his breath.

# NOW

## *2055 AS*

Scov charged, yelling indistinct sounds, the semblance of many curses and all the shapes of grief a mouth can form, knife out before him. A Priest of Dirt grabbed the tip of Scov's blade in a gloved hand, using it to seize the Nestler by the scruff of his neck.

Then, Jilo felt the twinges of being called home, of being offered a new way. Ka-Del's song calling. He couldn't describe what it sounded like, exactly, but it was as though a deep hum rumbled through his mind, a sign that the spear had not forgotten their bond. If he could locate it, he'd hear its call aloud, too, giving him the chance to steal it back from the Piatic cronies.

The hum led him to believe that the spear was somewhere beyond the hallway. Warm lantern glows echoed around the corner up ahead. He wasted no time.

The hound, gripping the lifeless body of Clev, did not see the full brunt of Jilo coming at it. A leather-braced knee drove into the beast's jaw, and Jilo swore he could hear it click out of place as the hound squealed in pain, flinging Clev's body across the hall and running down the stairs past him. The guards and priests, stunned at what had happened, clambered towards him and the one who now held Scov.

He leapt at the priest that held Scov, throwing his full weight against the man, so that the other priests and guards behind fell like a row of dominoes. Scov scuttled out of the priest's grip while Jilo made sure to stamp on each downed assailant's chest. He felt his leather boots break through rib and cartilage across most of the bodies, though he knew that they had little time. These guards were trained, and the Priests of Dirt were dangerous in their own right. They would be up again with haste, injured or not.

"Scov, quickly! Go right!" Jilo yelled over the sounds of anguish and the rising hum in his mind. He knew. Something in his heart, in his *soul*, told him Ka-Del was close at hand.

Down the hallway, several rooms became available to him and Scov, though he was hard-pressed to make a decision whilst behind him the sounds of clamouring men were growing closer.

"In here, Cousin Jilo!" Scov wheezed as he pushed through a dark door.

Jilo followed him in and smiled at his small friend. They had struck gold, or at least the dark blue hue of Ka-Del's cautioning glow. The spear had been put up on a workbench, clamps holding it in place. Jilo couldn't help but snigger. The Piatic noblemen who'd caught him had kept Ka-Del here, right beside the place where he'd been confined? Hours before, Ardyr had wagged it in his face tauntingly. Now, he would reclaim it. This spear was his heritage, his bloodline. It was all he had left of who he had been. Of his father and the people who'd raised him. He would've died in its pursuit.

"Scov, help me get it down," he breathed, looking over the clamps to find their handles. The jaws of the metal clamps were tight, and he felt close to rage that the spear had been treated this way.

Scov rammed his knife into the wall so that the door couldn't be opened from the other side. Then he leapt up onto the bench, holding onto one of the clamps. "Good Earth. Not good, Cousin Jilo," he said. "There are no handles to unwind these clamps."

Jilo snarled as the priests and guards found their way through the hall. They knew Jilo and Scov were in here, where Ka-Del's faint glow originated, and that small Izog knife wedged across the door wouldn't hold them back for long. No matter what happened next, the night was going to be filled with blood, Jilo was sure.

He felt around the darkness under the bench, hoping for a crate or box that might contain the handle they needed to uncrank the clamps. Nothing. He felt around the bench, which stretched around the room in a large U-shape. Nothing. Ka-Del was calling to him. He would not be whole again if he did not get the spear back. He already hadn't been whole for years.

This rescue mission wasn't supposed to take him and his friends to their deaths. But now, he wasn't so sure. If he paused for too long, thought for too long, the aches in his hands would return and the crusted-over ruins of his fingertips reminded him that Ka-Del was his only option for winning the fight. His father had breathed in Ka-Del's light, felt it, *used* it, whenever he had held the spear in his hands. Jilo was Hiro's son, but his abilities had always been inconsistent. Surely, with some more focus, he could do the same.

"Sing to me," he whispered, kneeling before the spear. "Sing to me, Ka-Del. Please. They'll kill us both if—"

The wall broke as the knife began to jut out from it. "Not long, Cousin Jilo!" Scov said, nervous. "There's nowhere for us to go!"

Jilo screamed in frustration and Scov darted into the opposite corner of the room, taken aback. "There is only one way this will go, Scov," he said through gritted teeth. "Either they die or we do. Now, help me rip out this bench!"

He yanked at the bench, which came away slowly from the other two benches that met its ends to circumference the room. It moved easier than he'd imagined it would, and it was lighter than he'd thought, too. Light enough to pick up, holding it out before him and Scov like a massive shield, Ka-Del strapped to its top like a bad omen for the enemy to see. He yelled a deep guttural cry, driving forward the spokes of adrenaline he needed to go through with his insane plan.

Then, he charged.

The bench rammed through the door's frame, splintering wood and breaking timber wall panels. He felt bodies succumb to the massive panel's force as he stepped on the leftovers, Scov in tow.

It became apparent that Jilo had no sense of direction while holding the bench out in front of him. If he hit an obstacle at this speed, he'd likely fracture his wrists, maybe break his arms.

"Keep moving, Cousin Jilo!" Scov yelled. "Scov will tell you where to go!"

Jilo felt the bench crash into a few more people, gritting at the force. His hands were getting tired, broken fingernails threatening to break his grip. The adrenaline that had carried him thus far was wearing thin. He breathed through the pain.

Suddenly, Scov cried, "Right, Jilo! Swing right!" He followed the instruction, noticing as he did so that he missed a large wooden beam that barricaded off the floor they were on from the one below. They had come to another staircase, and they needed to go down.

A sharp, whistling tone shot past Jilo's ear as he stood, affected by the stairs, not sure how to proceed. He glanced to his right, seeing an arrow firmly planted in the wall beside him. Below, the sounds of angry men filled the space, and another arrow slammed into the bench. He hoped Ka-Del was undamaged.

"They've got archers, Scov," Jilo said. "Climb onto my shoulder and look for me as I descend."

"Scov doesn't like this, Cousin Jilo," the small creature squeaked.

"I know, Scov, but this is our only chance." Beneath him, warm light trailed from where the enemy stood, bows in hand. The street was close if the lamplight could be seen from here. Jilo took a trembling step onto the first stair, keeping the bench top low enough to the ground that his boots were protected from potential arrow fire.

Scov peeked over the top of the bench every few moments before Jilo proceeded down another step. On the last three stairs, however, Jilo heard the first eerie crunch of timber splintering. The bench was getting heavier by the moment and judging by the thuds from the arrows, it was decorated with them.

Another crack sounded from the front of the board, and Jilo kept still. As long as they didn't move, the enemy couldn't hit them. Scov looked around the side of the bench. "Jilo! One of the clamps—Ka-Del is coming away from the wood!"

"Damn it!" Jilo swore. "We're stuck, Scov."

Another arrow *thunked* into the board, and Jilo felt the impact again. "Scov, do you have another blade?"

"Two." Scov nodded eagerly. "Always come prepared—"

"—with blades. Yes, I know." Jilo recalled the Great Hunts he'd been on with the Hidden Ones. If only he'd heeded the advice before today. "Can you sneak around me?" Jilo asked. "I can charge to the side, give you the chance to strike from behind. They'll be distracted."

"Fine," Scov said. "But don't you dare die, Cousin Jilo."

"Me?" Jilo suppressed a chuckle. "You're worried about me, the one with the wooden bench shielding my entire body from view?"

"Well, don't say Scov didn't warn you," the small creature said. Then he produced his two blades, each the size of a human switchblade. "Let's run!"

Jilo grabbed the bench, raising it enough that he could run without his feet hitting the wood from behind. He felt the board slam into a guard, then another. Scov was gone from sight and Jilo was exposed to the soldiers slowly surrounding him. Arrows pelted the wood rhythmically, allowing guards to get closer. Then, the squeak of a metal clamp coming undone caused Jilo's heart to pause. He felt the weight of Ka-Del swing from its place, smashing into the ground.

This was it. His final chance to escape lay with him now that Ka-Del was untethered. He groaned, heaving loudly as he tossed the bench out before him, leaping to the ground to retrieve Ka-Del. The second his hands gripped the spear, the familiar feeling of control eased into him, and he felt every pain in his body disappear. Light radiated from the spear across several hues and his vision changed, allowing him to see more clearly. Ka-Del had always been able to do things like this, improving his sensory responses in ways he'd never understood or, equally, never been able to replicate. The outline of each soldier was more obvious now, though the only light on this bottom floor came from the pollution of lamplight from the street outside. Large double doors lay ahead of him, and he could make out Scov's tiny frame pounding on guard after guard, slicing necks or stabbing.

His reflexes, suddenly more attuned with Ka-Del in hand, allowed him to whip around, catching two approaching guards in the throats as Ka-Del's shaft smacked them down. He ducked and wove between archers, who were too slow for his newly-refined focus. Eventually, he made his way to Scov, and they stood back-to-back, defending one another from what seemed like an endless swathe of attackers, all nestled within the building like infesting spiders in the dark.

"We've done it, Scov!" he breathed. He sliced Ka-Del's lotus-embossed spearhead across a man's thigh, sending him reeling to the ground, agonising barks clawing their way out of his throat. "We've done it!"

"Don't speak so soon, Cousin Jilo," Scov replied, leaping on a guard's face and slamming both his Izog knives into their eyes.

But he *would* speak so soon, he decided, because with Ka-Del in hand after years of separation, everything was fine. Every mountain felt conquerable with the spear in hand, every fight as though it was in his favour.

Then, as he finished off another guard, he felt the cold pull and tightening of a metal chain around his neck, and he dropped Ka-Del from the surprise of it.

Scov had been caught too, chains binding his torso, his furry paws caught under them. Two men held the chains, at least a head or so taller than Jilo and twice as wide.

They'd been caught from behind. Priests of Dirt marked the entrance to the building from the street side, awaiting them alongside another team of guards. Behind them, a gold-stamped carriage with three horses attached to its helm rested forebodingly on the cobbled streets of Piat.

"Bring them outside, and don't forget the grindel," spat one of the priests through their mask, an old, hollowed-out buffalo skull decorated with the blackened antlers of another kill. Jilo gritted his teeth as the chain around his neck was yanked tight, and he fell to the ground as his body was dragged out the door. He hated the term grindel. Ka-Del was no magician's trick.

He was surrounded by Priests of Dirt now, including those he had fought in the hallways earlier. They were exiting the building with what remained of the Ardyr's guards. The Piatic nobleman was nowhere to be seen.

At that very moment, the man in question somehow stepped out of the carriage, accompanied by a thinner person enveloped in a dark-brown cloak that hid their face, only the gentler outline of a woman's chin visible. Jilo couldn't understand how Ardyr, the rat, had gotten out of the building during the fight. And who was this that Ardyr had led here? Was it also their job to find Ka-Del? Priests of Dirt, he knew, came from Therador, not Piat. Just like the Nestlers had suspected, the Empire was very aware of Jilo's fight for Ka-Del, it seemed.

Jilo gulped, barely able to breathe as the guard's chain remained locked around his neck, pulling tighter if he showed any resistance.

"And who is this but our marauder of madness?" the unknown woman crooned. Jilo squeezed his eyes shut as firm but thin fingers seized his cheeks, digging into his stubble-dressed skin.

"This man is a southerner, my lady," the priest with the grim beard said.

"A southerner?" The words were barely above a whisper, her disbelief plain. "But they ... are all gone."

The priest grabbed Jilo's hair as the woman backed away from him like he was some kind of ghost. The priest's other hand slapped Jilo across the face, and he felt hot blood as his teeth bit down on his tongue.

"What is your name, Southerner? And how do you know about Ka-Del?" the priest asked gruffly.

To offer up the truth would be surrender, but to keep fighting ... What did he have to fight for now? After all this time spent separated from Ka-Del, only to watch the Empire seize it once more and abuse its power for their own gain? For years, Jilo had pursued his father's lost spear, hoping he could get it back and hold that which was his in his hands once more, to do those who suffered because of the Empire's thievery justice. But standing here, before the enemy ... This was the end.

Scov screamed from within the sack that had been tossed into the back of the cart. "Don't tell them, Cousin! Say nothing!"

Jilo shook his head. What was the point? They'd been caught, and they would surely go to their deaths. The Theradoran priests had Ka-Del, and Clev was dead.

"My name is Jilo, and Ka-Del was my father's spear." He spat every word, punctuating his failure.

The woman reached up two black gloves as if covering her mouth. Then she stepped forward into the streetlight and pulled down her cowl. The years had wearied her, but not as much as they should've. Her eyelids were lined with stiff crow's feet, but Jilo knew that face ...

"It cannot be ..." he whispered.

The woman's voice faltered on her next words. "L-little yam?"

Mother.

# THEN

## *1887 AS*

Violent waves moved Jilo quicker than an eel in a race. He felt his body slamming into trees, moving with masses of debris, plant-matter, and dirt through the raging river. If this water carried the Sickness, then he was doomed. But he held on, gasping between pockets of air and trying not to suck in any liquid as he was tossed around, beholden to the merciless tides. He could've let himself drown at any moment, but something felt wrong. *Something* told him it wasn't his time.

*Mother,* he thought, panicked. He'd practically been unconscious since the river's crazed tides had thrown themselves down upon Sai-Kathan. If he wasn't careful, he'd return to that state again. He put his arms across his face and let the water move him in whatever way it would, winding in and amongst the trees of the rainforest.

This was no ordinary river, and it was no ordinary Sickness. It started with people dying, their bodies corrupting as they faded from the world. But then it began to change the river itself, foaming the water even when the currents moved across sandy bottoms rather than rapids. In the last day, the water had increased in depth significantly—but it wasn't until it had grown like a deformed beast that the tribe's fears had truly come to fruition.

Then there was his father. Hiro was nowhere to be seen. And he'd let Jilo go to his mother alone. He wanted to scowl as he got washed into a clearing, the water's intensity reducing to something akin to a low current. He staggered as he got up, his body soaked in the poisonous water, debris all around. There was nobody else to be found.

He didn't have long, he decided, until his own skin would begin to fall away from his frame. Neither would anyone else, except maybe his father. Ka-Del might just be enough to keep the Sickness at bay. The holy spear had been marked by miracles for decades, becoming a symbol of nature's greatest and most mysterious gift: life. Though Jilo had seen it cleave betrayers, murderers, and other criminals, he had also seen the spear magically heal the bodies, hearts, and minds of many who touched it.

It could reveal the future, too, just like it had the previous night: dark blue for danger, and emerald for good. Nobody knew how Ka-Del could do these things. It was as though the next step towards logic and questioning defied reason. Faith alone kept Ka-Del in the hands of the Sai-Kathan. So maybe, just *maybe,* his father would live, and the spear would heal him completely.

But if it didn't … He shuddered at the memories that sputtered through his mind: melting skin, deformed bodies, and blood … the blood.

The water, it seemed, had stopped just shy of the clearing and was receding now, as though it was not allowed in this place. It turned out, as Jilo walked through the mushy, sodden grass, that he was headed uphill in a direction that the exploding river could not muster up the energy to overcome.

He was surprised to find that, although he had been bathed in the sick water, he felt fine. Tired, yes, and battered? Bruised? Of course. But he didn't feel any other symptoms. Shallow breath, he recalled, was one of the first signs. Then the eyes would slump in their sockets as though they could not be held in place, and the face began to sag. Finally, as the breathing became more haggard and forced, the body would start to fall apart. People who were at the end looked like scarecrows: sticks upon which hung the drabs and scraps of clothing, blowing in the breeze.

He moved further from the clearing, mindful of the incline. He had to find somewhere to rest, away from the river. He needed …

Water. All that drinking water his father and he had scoured for, gone in the chaos. He didn't remember dropping the bag.

As the trees began to darken, the black of night no longer allowing the moon to glance voyeuristically down on him, he realised he was *very* alone. *Mother. Father. Where are you?*

The fourteen-year-old heir to a once-mighty tribe of Kathani slouched under a palm tree, cupped his face in his hands, and sobbed. Sleep came, eventually, in the folds of his final thoughts. *Night, take me. Take me while I cannot feel it.*

---

Jilo awoke the next morning to the song of the skyswallows, wonderfully alive. Fatigued, maybe, and wet, certainly. But he was alive. He was breathing the fresh dawn air, and he pinched the skin on his arm, noticing how it clung to his bones. That was when he rolled over in the thick, rugged grass and caught the edges of a glow, faint through the long, verdant blades.

He gasped, plunging his hands into the grass and flattening it so he could see what was hidden beneath. Ka-Del lay in the grass, glimmering green. The long wooden handle, the lotus flowers inlaid across the metal spearhead ... His father's spear had somehow found its way to him. He knew the spear was magical, an artefact of the oldest Q'aran humans, beginning with Ne-Lo the Visionary and passing through line after line until it had reached his father. But he had not known it was capable of finding its way home; not like this, at least.

He grasped it and pressed it to his forehead, the cool grey of the polished but knotted burls connecting him to his past, the kind of happiness that used to preside over his life before the Sickness had come.

He slowly grew cognisant of the scene around him, however. The remnants of his people lay strewn about, and in the daylight, he saw the chaos for what it was. He stood, his stomach growling and his throat dry, despite the wet cold of his skin and hair. Seeing the sun at its low point in the east told him which way he needed to go, and how long he had to get there before nightfall. Tel-Kathan was a hard day's hike through the rainforest, or two days at a lighter pace. Though he'd been there before, he had barely been eight years old at the time. Rei-Kathan was even further to the south, and he'd never been. All he could do was go north and hope for the best.

*Mother.* The thought of her brought to his heart an ache like a hammer blow against iron. Where was she? If she was dead, it was because of him. *"Do what it is that you should do."*

His father's words rang in his ears as he stifled a sudden sob, his tears first a trickle, and then an open faucet as fast as the River Tomei at its most violent, its most ... alive.

All he had was this spear and the wet clothes pressed into his back, constant reminders of what his people had suffered the night before. There was no telling the gravity of death that had taken place. Thousands of people suddenly swept away.

Here one minute, gone the next. What right did he, the fourteen-year-old remnant of a once-powerful tribe, have to be alive and well? The Sickness would take him. If it would not, maybe he would take himself.

The forest twisted and turned, an indecipherable, patternless expanse of sinewy trees, moist undergrowth, and mixed cacophonies of birdsong and cricket call. Though the summer sun swung blows at the canopy before it reached him, its grandeur could still be felt as he sweated so profusely, even the temperature could not dry the clothes on his back. Occasionally, the odd sounds of scampering wildlife or slithering snakes threatened to turn him back. But towards what? He had no home, no reason to turn around. Forward was all he had left.

At one point, the forest broke in its density, and he saw in the distant northwest the looming Great Tree of Aobia. He considered it in its glory, arching above all else in the forest, and dismissed it entirely. The tree-dwellers would reap the best of the earth and never be privy for a moment to the destruction his people had endured. He turned his head dismissively and travelled forth.

Around noon, his stomach moaned like a gelded calf, and he took it as a sign that the Sickness had not yet taken him. How lucky he was to want for food, to feel the need for sustenance complimented by the desire for it.

Suddenly, the hand holding Ka-Del started burning, and he glanced down at his father's spear. The same opulent glow radiated around it, though now it was so blue, he had to squint to see the blade through the light. *Danger?* he thought, tensing his shoulders. His wrist jerked, and the end of the spear pointed in a particular direction. *Food perhaps, and this way!* He could practically feel its message. A creature was only dangerous if it could not be bested. But Jilo had a spear, and with it, he would make whatever it was Ka-Del was warning him about his next meal.

He had known the power of Ka-Del only through his father. Now, he could wield it and see the peculiar object for what he had known it to be—a mysterious artefact of great power. Power that was not yet meant for him. He felt a mixture of guilt and hope as he led himself through the forest in the direction the spear tip seemed to be gesturing towards. If he could not find Tel-Kathan, maybe Ka-Del could.

Around a tangled mess of trunks, he came to his first meal and lunged. A clean, ripe selection of lotus. He usually hated the stuff uncooked, though his mother had chided him for it. But now he knew why she'd told him to never complain. Now, he had nothing. Nothing but this grace-saving spear and these lotuses.

He pulled the flowers out at their roots, discarding their buds back into the watery earth they had lain in. The roots were muddy and wet, but they were vital, crunchy, and a reminder of his purpose. He made a sour face as he scoffed two of them before stashing a few more in the folded pockets of his long pants. His feet squelched as he left the shallow lotus pond, not once looking back.

Ka-Del had faded again. Maybe its mission was complete. Jilo looked at the sun, nervous at how far across the sky it had progressed. Already it was beginning its swift descent. It would not be long before he would be stuck here, in the dark, exposed to the secrets the forest kept. He wasn't supposed to know what went on in this place. He should have been helping his mother prepare dinner, retrieve the clothes that had been washed and dried by the river, or casting dice with his friends. He should have been able to retreat safely to his tent and his scrolls at the end of the day.

The realisation of it only furthered his panic, and he ran, jogging where he could or walking quickly where he had to, trying to find his way through the forest.

It did not end. Hours passed. Night came. Still, he was a fourteen-year-old boy who had abandoned his duty, lost his family and his people, and had no idea what to do in the foreign place that surrounded him now.

Jilo held Ka-Del tight that night as he sank into the soft roots of an old pan-din palm and cowered before the darkness. For the first time, he felt like nothing. A predator could pick him off, and nobody would hear him scream. If something happened to him, would Ka-Del listen? Would he even survive the night free of the Sickness?

His only comfort was the echo of his mother's words from when she had comforted him as a child. Jilo had never been one to sleep soundly. Terrors had afflicted him from a young age, causing him to scream, scream, *scream* until his parents had raced to his corner of the tent.

*"We create our reality, little yam,"* came the soothing voice of his mother. He deepened his breaths, tuning his ears inwards, away from the ambience of the forest. *"If we can create that, then we can dream of anything we want. Do not yield to the nightmares, Jilo."*

Tears pricked the edges of his tired eyes, and he squeezed them shut, trying to keep his breaths steady. He listened to his mother: calming. Assuring.

*"Now sleep, little yam. Sleep, and let the dream fill you."*

# NOW

## *2055 AS*

JILO SAT, HANDS CHAINED behind his back, in the carriage that his mother had arrived in. Scov had been taken by another set of priests when he and his mother had been scooped up and into the carriage.

Talei sat before him, clearly still as shocked by his appearance as he was by hers. Surrounding them were Priests of Dirt in their ominous skull masks. They neither spoke nor moved their heads. In fact, Jilo wondered whether they had heads at all or if they were the reanimated corpses of Therador's finest.

"How long until we reach the Hall?" his mother asked the priests in the driver's seat.

"Half an hour," one replied, his gruff voice muffled by the mask he sported. That skull had been a human's once, before it had been fused with the antlers of a deer and fashioned into the shape it now bore. Jilo shivered at the thought as his mother patted his knee.

"I still cannot believe you're alive," Mother said. They'd been moving through the quiet nighttime streets of Piat for a short while now, and his mother had only just ceased crying. But despite the surprise he'd felt from seeing her, he couldn't help but wonder at the darker matter at hand. Why was his mother here with Priests of Dirt from Therador, in pursuit of Ka-Del? And how was she *alive* after all these years, let alone the Sickness that had claimed the rest of his people?

He must've been focusing his eyes on her long enough for his mother to furrow her brows. "Are you all right, little yam?"

He pursed his lips. "What are you doing here, Mother? And how?"

She had aged, but the crow's feet that tugged at her wet eyes should've been longer, deeper; her hair should've been greyer, her skin looser. One hundred sixty-seven years since he'd seen his mother. A long time for a human to live, he knew. But his people had always been special that way; they lived as long as the Aobians in the Great Tree. His mother, however, must have been nearly two centuries old by now.

"I woke up the morning after the flood, all those years ago," she began, "and I was alive. I couldn't believe the river hadn't taken me. Or that the Sickness hadn't claimed me. But there I was, totally and utterly alive, somewhere in the forest." She sighed, eyes suddenly wet again. "I looked for you, little yam. You *and* your father."

It was Jilo's turn to look away. He could say nothing.

Mother reached up and cupped his chin, raising his eyes to hers like she'd done when he had been a boy. How could so much time pass, and yet none at all?

"Little yam, please tell me. Your father, is he—"

"Mama," Jilo said, pushing her hand away. "He is gone."

She let out a sob, and Jilo wondered whether he should comfort the estranged parent that sat before him.

"How long?"

Jilo's frown deepened at the question and the memory it brought back to life, like the stoking of an emberfire. He felt the sting of tears upon his own eyes. "One hundred and sixty-seven years," he said through a clenched jaw. He felt the pain of every year that had passed as tears blurred his vision. He would not cry. He would hold it back. He would—

Mother leant into him then, pressing her forehead to his. At that moment, the hard exterior he had grown to seal in all his emotions broke, the skin beneath touching the skin of his parent. The tears became too hard to contain. The smell of his mother was no different after all these years. The sound of her tears and the rhythm of her weeping were familiar. For the first time in a long time, he wasn't alone. There was togetherness in the suffering, commonplace found amidst the wracking grief. He didn't have to do this by himself.

But as the sounds of their anguish died, he sat back up in his seat, feeling the brunt of reality's fist. Nothing changed the fact that on both sides of him were Priests of Dirt, minions of the tyrannical Theradoran Empire. And even more, his mother was the one in charge.

She looped her hair behind both her ears and sniffed. Their eyes locked onto one another, intent with the desire to know why they were both in this situation. "Why are you here?" He tried to hide the edge in his voice, but it came out nonetheless. She was not the same mother he had known as a child. And he was not the same child. Here, now, he was a prisoner.

Mother took a moment to consider her words, resting her chin on her palms. "Ka-Del was brought here to the Piatic noblemen for ... important experiments, Jilo. I've taken care of it ever since it came into my hands—"

"You?" Jilo snapped, cutting her off. "*Your* hands? All this time, you've had our family heirloom? And you did not think to find *me*?" An odd pain seized him, a tremor in the chest. His breathing became flighty. He had been left alone, with no kin left to care for him. All these years had gone by, and she hadn't thought to come looking for him. He remembered the night Ka-Del had been taken from him.

"*Leave the boy. He'll freeze in these woods before morning comes.*"

"*But sir. He is a southerner. A Kathani boy, here, in the Hidden Forest?*"

"*It's none of our business who he is, Brother. Our business is the spear. And we've got it now. We've let enough blood run tonight; I wouldn't dare provoke these feral creatures any more than we already have. Pack up your men; we're going home.*"

Jilo would never forget the priest who'd led that insurgency crew. He'd donned the skull of a wolf with tusks forced into the ear cavities, and had muscles as thick as the tree that Jilo had hidden behind, barely metres away. He'd worn crudely fashioned brown leather armour with a black cloak, and the stamp of a deer head upon the chest. The Theradoran Empire had razed the edges of the Greenwood outside the Hidden Forest, decimated the population of Nestlers and Burrowers alike, and taken the last thing Jilo had held close.

Now, he sat with his mother after years apart, more than were natural for most people. Time seemed to have severed their connection. Even blood wasn't privy to the slow toil of years. Jilo was barely who he had been as a boy. He was less Kathani and more of a Hidden One now, despite the marked differences between his anatomy and theirs. And his mother was less Kathani and more ... everyone's enemy. The empire that had started this war. The nation that sought power over Q'ara and its many peoples.

"I did not send the command that night for Ka-Del to be taken. Not in that manner," his mother said through anguished gasps. "And if I had known you were there, I would've brought you home. I swear it, little yam. *I swear it* on Ne-Lo's Founding Verses."

"You know nothing of the Founding Verses!" Jilo bit back. "Our people are gone, and you have made yourself a maiden of the enemy. Therador started this war. Now, we fight and humble them once more. Centuries of tension since Settlement, Mother. When will this bloodshed end?"

"I am no maiden of Therador," his mother yelled, surprising him. "I carry Therador's blood in me. So do you, child."

He frowned as his mother nodded to the two Priests of Dirt sitting on either side of him. They took his arms in punishably tight grips as she went on speaking. "Now listen to me and listen well. Therador has been on the cusp of learning to harness the power of Luminosity for years. The last time we tried, the queen of Aobia, who'd traded with us, was caught and killed and the monarchy was overturned. That republic of tree-dwellers is keeping their power secret when it should be shared and used for all our benefit. Imagine a world where we could access the same connection to the earth, the same network of life that they can. We could do anything, things we've never been able to imagine. Heal the sick, remove pain from the human experience completely, *free* ourselves from death! We wouldn't need empires, or kingdoms like Adira. We could be one people, like we were before Settlement. Ka-Del is the key to that, Jilo. I will not have you take it away from me again. I would've inherited it from your father anyway when the time was right."

She straightened her robes, and her face became suddenly serious, if not angered, in a way entirely unfamiliar to Jilo. "So, I'll give you two options and may Ne-Lo and the gods favour your choice. Stay with me and fight for what is true and good. Equal access to Luminosity for all. Or go and never let me see your traitorous face again. Because I *will destroy* you if you continue to interfere."

His face burned. This was his mother. The person who had held him as a baby, cuddled him as a child, dressed him, fed him, *taught* him to be who he was. Now, she felt like a stranger, entirely detached from the life she had once shared with him. Was she the same person on any level at all? The world around him withered like a cluster of tangled facades, all falling apart and coming back together again.

He didn't know her. He didn't know anything.

"I will not go with you," he whispered, bowing his head as the grips on his arms tightened.

"Very well," his mother said, lifting her chin. "With my heart's fullest regret, child, we go our separate ways. Once and for all." She looked at her priests. "Throw him out."

"Yes, Talei," one of the priests replied. Immediately, he was gathered up and tossed, like a limp bundle of sticks, out of the speeding carriage. He hit the dusty ground of Piat, tasted blood, and groaned.

The particular street Jilo lay upon was a narrow cobblestone path that ran parallel to the main stretch of road running through Piat's heart. Even now, he tasted sand. Sand in his nose, sand in his mouth. He hated sand, he decided. The stuff got everywhere.

He rolled to the side of the road, hugging his ribs with bandaged hands, hands his mother had bandaged. Ka-Del was gone. Clev, a Nestler who had been among the few who had looked after him when he'd first come to be in the Hidden Forest, was dead. Clev's nephew, Scov, might be alive, but Jilo had no idea where he would be. They were both as foreign to this city as to one another.

It was a miracle that the little Nestler somehow found him lying in the gutter, his heart thudding in his ears, his forced breaths letting out groans with each exhalation.

"Cousin Jilo!" came Scov's voice as a tiny body landed on him, furry paws turning Jilo's face to look up.

"Aren't I happy to see you?" Jilo said, smiling through the pain he'd sustained when he'd first hit the ground.

"Scov can say the same." The small, weasel-like creature looked at him with wide eyes. "Not more injuries, Cousin?"

"A cracked rib, perhaps, but I'll live," Jilo croaked before coughing as Scov yanked on his arm, trying to help him up. The small creature handed Jilo a cake of some kind, which he'd kept stashed in his satchel.

"Human bakeries will never cease to distract Scov," he said. "That woman, she was your mother?"

Jilo brushed sand off his shoulder. "Yes," he murmured, breaking a piece off the spiced cake and wolfing it down as he spoke. "My mother is from Therador, as it turns out. I never knew that." All his life, he'd known that his mother didn't look entirely like other Kathani—her skin was a shade more olive than tan, and her eyes were deep black wells. Her nose was prominent, but he'd always found it endearing. She was *his* mother. It hadn't mattered that she looked different.

Now, however, it did. Because it signified something worse than he'd realised. He was the child of the enemy in this war they fought. The Four-Front War had taken from humanity, the Hidden Ones, and the Aobians for years now. Piat and Sethiliquin had banded together with Therador while Adira took cover in the east, protected only by the expanse of hills known as the Outfields. Ghabbat, in the north, did what they could to assist, but the valleys they needed to cross into Adiran territory kept their forces slowed to a trickle. Aobia, the Great Tree, helped from a distance, sending people only when it was required. He gritted his teeth. The tree-dwellers were said to be the original people of this land, and yet they did nothing to look after any of it that lay outside of the Tree's shade.

Scov must've noticed Jilo's mind drift and coughed to catch his attention. "Cousin Jilo, Scov knows we failed. We should've taken Ka-Del and kept Clev from death. But that is in the past. We must continue to fight. Do not let this revelation break you."

Jilo stared at his friend. Sighing, he nodded. "I know, Scov. I just need a moment." In this back-alley street, not even the leaves of the palms rustled. Everything was still and quiet. Though Piat's class divide meant there were homeless sprawled throughout the city streets, this one was empty of human activity save for Jilo. For the first time in a while, he could breathe.

They'd come to Piat—he and Clev and Scov—at the command of Sergeant Cavtil, a Nestler elder who commanded the army at the Adiran Outfields now and answered only to the circle of elders in the Hidden Forest. The elders had only hesitantly admitted the Hidden Ones to join the war effort, and Cavtil had taken up the initial orders with another sergeant, an older and more begrudging elder known as Garv. Once they'd caught wind of Ka-Del being used to heal people in Piat, they hadn't hesitated to send Jilo on his way. He had one simple job: retrieve his heirloom and bring it back to the Hidden Forest for safeguarding. Nobody, including him, knew the breadth of Ka-Del's power. But he knew that Therador was the last nation on all of Q'ara he would pick to have it.

Clev had left his wife and children, while Scov had left his promised, a Nestler known as Yva. Jilo knew how much he wanted to go home. No matter the cost, he'd promised he would make that happen. Now that Ka-Del had been taken and Clev killed, he wasn't so sure.

"You say words that are different than those that are in your mind, Cousin," Scov whispered.

"Scov, don't you want to go home? Hold Yva once more and live a good, long life?"

Scov chuckled. "Scov wants nothing more. But Scov is also a realist, Cousin. If we go back, we go without honour. And without honour, we are lifeless. It is our blood, Cousin."

"I wish this wasn't my lot, sometimes," Jilo replied.

"And what? You'd rather sit back, watch this war ravage our people from afar?" Scov shook his head. "That is not how this life works. Keep honour close. Keep *blood* close."

Jilo nodded. He was exhausted. But Scov was right. He sniffed and began to rise to his feet. "What's next, Scov? Ka-Del is gone, likely back to Therador."

"Ah, but that's the thing, Cousin," Scov squeaked. "When Scov escaped the priests, Scov followed the carriage that brought you here. When Scov was at the bakery a couple streets away, Scov spotted an old friend entering a public house."

"An old friend?" Jilo asked. "Do I know him?"

Scov shrugged. "Maybe. But he is the greatest scavenger known to my people. If anyone can find Ka-Del, it is Barsh the Burrower."

# THEN
## *1887 AS*

IT HAPPENED THE DAY the summer died. A now-homeless boy from Sai-Kathan, orphaned and forced into cold, dark places to survive.

"*Little yam, where are you?*" *The voice came from the darkest corners of the earth.*

*Try as he might, the boy knew not where her voice came from, knew not how to find her in this infinite, enveloping darkness.* "*Mama?*"

*But no one answered. The cold darkness came creeping in. Claws emerged, shining beacons in the black, reaching for him, holding him, tearing him apart. A homeless, lonely boy in the throes of the unknown would take his final breaths.*

*And nobody would hear them.*

Jilo awoke with a gasp, the nightmare from the past few nights tormenting his sleep again. He lay in a makeshift vine-bound hammock beneath two zhate trees. Below him, pools of meat and flesh reeked. The only place he'd found close to the River Tomei, which he could follow north to Tel-Kathan, was where some of his people must've perished only days before in the flood. Bones were strewn across the ground. But the flesh ... It sickened him to think of what had happened to those who had died of the water poisoning. Meat falling from bones like slow-cooked chicken. Why hadn't he died, too? And what had saved him? Was it Ka-Del, or something else?

He was so tired. Every time he tried to sleep, he woke, either gagging from the smell of the flesh pooled beneath him or from the nightmare. The events repeated in his mind: Mother crying for him as the water parted around her, her fingernails snapping against the rocks, her body sliding in the mud created by the river. Her anguish was a hint of what her last moments must have looked like. What if it was *her* skin that was mushed all over the forest floor?

He held Ka-Del tight every night, hoping it would bring him peace. Sometimes, when he was walking, the spear hummed, a low drone that nearly went unnoticed. His father had never mentioned this, and he'd never heard the sound before. But he was certain it came from the spear after he'd sat in a grassy clearing the day before and felt its call.

It had only been earlier in the day that the oddest thing had happened. The spear had shown him a vision while he'd walked in the woods. He'd seen his mother, alive and well, in a dark place, surrounded by stone walls. She'd been older and dressed in black robes. He'd seen his father crying by the river, mourning the loss of his people. It had not mattered what the images had been or what the spear had intended by showing them to him. They'd sent chills down Jilo's spine as confusion had interrupted the grieving he'd already begun for both his parents. When he'd continued on his way, the sound of Ka-Del had become stifled amidst nature's sonorous layers, and he'd forgotten all about the incident until now, when he woke up again, sweating and clinging to the spear.

He was completely awake, but the sun would not rise for hours yet. Though he hated walking in the dark, the idea of getting started on his trek before the heat of the day motivated him. His travel slowed every time he fell under the sun's glare. He would try to find pond water, build a fire, and boil it in coconut shells, slowly so they wouldn't burn. Coconuts were rife in this part of the forest, but many were meaty, offering food rather than liquid. All things considered, he wasn't doing too badly. He knew the basics of survival. That was how the Kathani people lived: one with the land and ever-roaming. But he couldn't endure another day of the sun or the muggy, mosquito-ridden forest.

Jilo swung out of the hammock. He clutched Ka-Del and felt it pulse with its usual mix of blue, green, and purple light. Then he reached for his small bag, a flimsy thing he'd woven out of vines over the past two nights. There wasn't much inside: a handful of dried berries, some burnt fragments of pan-din root, and the dried remains of a couple frogs. He chewed the pan-din root unenthusiastically as he waltzed off into the slow beginnings of the morning after packing his meagre belongings.

The sounds of the forest were acute: leaves rustling, birds singing, and water rushing in the distance. The density of life was quickly growing thicker, and Jilo squinted through treetops to check that he was moving in the right direction. However, with the sun yet to rise, he would need to use his intuition.

As he walked, he considered how far he'd come since the Sickness had wiped out Sai-Kathan. He'd moved as fast as he could these past four days, but he had grown tired over the last two. Perhaps, he'd travelled thirty ri or so, but he feared if that was the case, he was likely another week away from Tel-Kathan. He tried not to think about it. Another week out here could be enough to end him. The summer heat ate at him slowly, like a multi-course feast. If he did not find a place to rest for a day, he may shrivel up and die.

He paused at a cluster of mushrooms growing from a fallen zhate trunk, and his stomach grumbled. These would be edible, the same kind as those his mother had cooked with. They had tiny caps and grew in formation on long stems. Cooked with lard and bean paste, they tasted incredible on top of a bowl of fresh rice. Tears sprung to his eyes. His mother's cooking was something he would miss more than he could have ever guessed.

He bent to pluck the clumps of mushrooms from their dock when he heard the crack of a branch from somewhere ahead, accompanied by the flickering of light against the trees. Not the moon, but something shiny. Someone else was here. He went completely still, listening with his breath held. Nothing. Whoever they were, they knew he was near, too.

Three figures emerged through the foliage, barely taller than the surrounding bushes. Jilo couldn't make out who they were, but they definitely weren't human. He shivered, stopping where he stood so as to not alert them to his presence. If he stayed still, maybe they wouldn't notice him. The figures were furry with small ears. The flicker of light appeared again, and he caught the outline of something sharp through the leaves. Was this a family of hyo cats ready to pounce upon their night prey? If so, he was as good as dead.

He gulped, his heartbeat rising. They were close enough now that he couldn't move a muscle. The snap of a twig or crunch of a leaf would be enough to tip off his location.

*La!* he cursed silently. He squeezed his eyes shut as he realised the obvious. Ka-Del glowed a dull green in his hand, subtly so but enough to get the creatures' attention. At least it wasn't blue. Either these creatures were not here to hurt him or they still didn't know he was there.

"What is that light, Cousin?" said one of the creatures. It sounded feminine, but it was unlike any human voice he'd heard, scratchier and breathier. The whisper cut through the silence like the sharp shape that continued to flicker, reflecting the moonlight.

Not teeth, knives. Furry creatures holding knives.

Hidden Ones from the Hidden Forest, north of where he was now. What were they doing here? The Hidden Ones were an old race, older than the Aobians, and they lived only in the Hidden Forest, a mysterious part of Southern Q'ara that was as hard to stumble through as it was to spot the creatures when doing so. For them to be out here, in the south, was unexpected.

"I see her," another said. "It's a human girl. Maybe she's lost, Cousins."

*Girl?* Jilo wore his hair long, as was customary in the Kathani tribes. But he looked like no girl. He frowned.

"Look what you've gone and done, Cavtil. You've angered the small thing!" The third voice was gravelly, like wet riverstones grinding together.

"Shut up, Clev. Maybe she's related to the other one we found. They look similar, don't they?"

"Dear human child," the feminine one purred. "Are you lost, here in the forest? Where are your parents?"

Jilo clamped his mouth shut. What would they do if he spoke? Would they take him away with them, back to their Hidden Forest? Did Hidden Ones even like humans?

Hot in his hand, Ka-Del began to shine brighter, a deep blue aura about it that he could not mistake. The colour of warning.

That had been how he and his father had known they'd been doomed.

He put the spear out before him, the tip of it on guard. "Do not come closer," he said. "I am armed."

"Armed?" The one called Cavtil chuckled.

"It's a boy," the female said.

"Yes, Zya," Clev cut her off. "Child, that stick is no match for three of us. Do you not know that you have been discovered by the Hidden Ones?"

"What do you want with me?" Jilo asked. "I am just a boy. I've done nothing to you. Please leave me alone. I'll leave this place, never to return. I promise."

Cavtil sighed. "Let's take him back with us, Cousins. It cannot be a coincidence that we've come across two humans this night."

Jilo snarled and leapt from the bushes, Ka-Del still in hand. He would not go quietly. He had a mission, a chance to find Tel-Kathan, and, maybe, the remnants of his people. "No!" he cried, as a great net made of vines was unfurled by the three Hidden Ones, falling over him. He thrashed about to escape it, letting Ka-Del drop to the ground as the net tightened around him. They bound his ankles and took up his father's spear.

Then they dragged him across the rough and bumpy forest floor. They did not say a thing despite his protests and shouts for help.

It didn't take long for them to reach their campsite, Jilo in tow, netted up. They tossed him beside a pile of packs, tiny bedrolls and tools, and there he lay, unable to escape, while the tiny weasel-like creatures scampered into the bushes carrying Ka-Del with them. He looked around, trying to see if he was alone, but the sun was only just beginning to rise, and he couldn't distinguish the plants from animals in the dimness of dawn.

Something shuffled, a great lump on the ground to his right that he'd just noticed, cloaked by the shadows of a clump of trees. It grunted and began to grow in size, a rising black void. Shivers ran down his back as he squinted, trying to make out whatever features he could of the figure.

It was standing now, swaying as though it had only one foot. It hopped toward him, the edges of the dawnlight illuminating its shape so that Jilo could see the rope binding the figure's ankles. He followed his eyes to the shape's head and widened them in disbelief.

Hiro, his father, was alive.

"My son." Hiro said the words in his once stoic voice, now broken.

Jilo felt tears creep up to the surface. "I … thought you were dead. You just … left me?"

"Left you?" His father's voice grew an edge as he leant over Jilo, trying to get a good look at him. "I would never leave you or your mother." Hiro's green eyes stared at him, challenging Jilo to respond.

"Mother, is she—"

"Gone," Hiro said, looking away. Jilo thought he heard a sob, like a sharp inhale, but he could not make out his father's expression. "So," Hiro went on, turning back to him. "The weasels caught you too?"

"Where are we, Father?" Jilo whispered, replying to Hiro with another question. "Will they kill us?"

Hiro snorted. "Kill us? No. They like to claim they are vicious and undefeatable because they spend so much of their time away from the rest of us. But they can't kill us."

"They think we can't kill them, Cousins!" The voice of Clev, one of Jilo's captors, came chortling through the trees, carrying a long leather wrap. "The humans should be thankful we are securing our hunt so that they can share in it."

"If we can keep them alive," added Cavtil, emerging from the trees with a number of other Hidden Ones, "we can kill them just as well. Let them make their choice, Cousins." He turned to face Hiro and Jilo. Jilo was surprised that, even lying on the ground in a tangle of netting, he was at the height of Cavtil's head. "Every year, the Nestlers and Burrowers of the Hidden Forest spread out across the bushland of Q'ara to embark on a Great Hunt. Every year, we take back the greatest prize we can catch and feast together. Already, those of us who hunted in the Greenwood of the Hidden Forest will be dining and awaiting our return. Perhaps our greatest prize this hunt was not game, but humans. Will you come back with us and make your friendship known to our elders? Or will you die here, filled with the persistent hubris of your race, unable to see that you are both alone and nobody will find you or take you in?"

Jilo gulped under his father's hard stare. Clev unrolled the leather he'd been carrying from behind Cavtil, letting Ka-Del thud into the earth. Its hue, Jilo noted, was no longer a dark and eerie blue, but instead the vibrant green it usually was when his father held it.

"My spear," Hiro said. "You have my spear?"

Cavtil shook his head. "The child had your spear, human. We seized it when we found him. If you are its owner, then it is rightfully yours." Cavtil reached down to pick up the spear, which was at least thrice as tall as the weasel. Without hesitation, he swung it down on Hiro's ankles, slicing the binding cleanly through the middle. If Jilo had attempted the same thing, he would have surely missed. Maybe these weasels were more formidable than he'd first thought.

Hiro lunged forward, snatching Ka-Del from Cavtil's paws like it was the only thing which kept him alive. A fire lit in him, the same that Jilo knew his father had carried his whole life. Ka-Del ... did something to him. Made him stronger and more confident. It also made him sharp and unpredictable. Hiro stepped over Jilo's small frame, forcing Ka-Del's spearhead into the nets, ripping them apart so Jilo could clamber out.

"You have my respect, Cavtil, Nestler of the Greenwood," Hiro said. "For returning Ka-Del into my hands, I thank you. The boy and I will come with you. And when the time is right, we will find our people. Somewhere out here, in the endless green." Then he peered at Jilo, and Jilo noticed his father's grip tighten around Ka-Del's handle. It did not matter that Jilo was the one who had brought the spear here. It was not his.

And it never would be.

# NOW

## *2055 AS*

"Ah, iffid isn' Scov the Nestler!" Barsh proclaimed, slamming a steel tankard down on the tabletop, spilling foamy ale everywhere. "Whad brings you 'ere, tree-climber? Haven't seen you since the last hunt all those years ago."

"Barsh," Scov said, nodding at the other Hidden One. Barsh had a different face to those Jilo had grown used to seeing. Burrowers weren't commonly above ground in the Greenwood. Their tunnel systems were complex and innumerable, and that seemed to work for them. Barsh's eyes, as a result, reflected light more easily than Scov's, indicated by the bright flame of the lantern before him on the table, floating in the centre of both irises. His claws were long, growing from even longer fingers. His fur was mangier compared to Scov's soft coat. Lastly, his ears flopped down with an odd lilt, but Jilo couldn't recall seeing a

Burrower with ears like that. It must've just been because Barsh was drunk.

"And thissss," Barsh slurred while slouching in his seat with a single paw gesturing towards Jilo. "Thisss is the 'uman boy, ain't it? The Greenwood child?"

"Yes, Barsh," Scov said, wriggling into a seat at the table. "And we need your help, sadly."

"Ah, shidouddaluck," Barsh said, hanging his head and shaking it slowly. "Barsh is all worked up, unfortunad-e-ly." He started to laugh a mad, deep chortle.

"Scov needs you to listen to us, Barsh!" Scov snapped, grabbing Barsh by the shoulders. "This is serious!"

Barsh took a moment to process what Scov was saying. He opened his mouth and Jilo winced before the words came out. Then he stifled a laugh himself when all that left Barsh's mouth was a long, guttural belch, right in Scov's direction. "Barsh can listen," he said. "Learned to do that after my grandfather disappeared off the west coast of Q'ara!"

Jilo frowned. "What?"

Scov shook his head as Barsh went on. "Los' my granddaddy to the high seas. Didn't lis'en, see? Ended up on a pirate ship looking for hidden is-lands. Never saw 'im again." He dropped his head sullenly.

"I-lands," Scov corrected. "They're called i-lands, drunk fool."

"Thassss right!" Barsh chuckled, perking back up. "Islands. What was Barsh thinking? So anyway, whaddya want Barsh to do?"

"A Theradoran noblewoman has stolen a very important Hidden Object," Scov explained. "A spear known as Ka-Del."

"It belonged to my father," Jilo said.

"What's so speshial about this spear?" Barsh asked.

Jilo tightened his lips, but Scov spoke. "It is Luminous."

"A grindel?" Barsh gasped.

"Don't call it that," Jilo snapped. "I hate that word." Grindel was a term that seemed to have originated with the Empire as they'd sought Luminous objects over the years. It was a reduction of the natural beauty of Q'ara and the secrets it contained. Ka-Del, Jilo was sure, was one of them. He'd seen things in that spear for years, and now some of them were coming to fruition.

"You want to reclaim it?" Barsh asked. "Which noblewoman has it?"

Scov sighed. Jilo knew it was his turn to answer. "My mother," he said.

"Your—what?" Barsh exclaimed.

"I thought she was dead, years ago," Jilo explained. "But she was the one who captured me. She sent Priests of Dirt after us, and they killed Clev."

"*Killed Clev?*" Barsh cried, aghast. He pressed a paw to his mouth in shock.

"Shh!" Scov cried. "Grief is deserved, Barsh, but not so loudly. And not now. Now, we have work to do."

Jilo swallowed before going on. "I would do anything to bring Clev back. But it is an impossible wish. All we can do to avenge him is fight and retrieve Ka-Del from the Empire's hands."

Barsh held his gaze with dark, beady eyes. "Where will we find the spear?" Something changed in the Burrower's stare, hardness coming over him. A shade of anger, quiet as stone. This was a fierce Hidden One, and Jilo knew at that moment Scov had chosen wisely to seek his help.

"My mother was thoughtless enough to reveal where she and the priests were going, a place called the Hall. Ka-Del will be there." Maybe Mother wouldn't, but at least that would prevent Jilo from inflicting her with harm. He still hadn't lived down the shock of seeing her with the Theradoran priests, but he had suppressed it to do what was necessary.

"Hmm ... Barsh thinks he knows what that is. There is a place near here called the Piatic Hall of the Dead." The mercenary Burrower stroked his furry chin.

Jilo tapped his fingers on the table. "Where is it?"

"The question isn't 'where is it?', man-child," Barsh said, smiling. "It's, 'what's in there?'"

"What are you talking about, Barsh?" Scov asked, impatient.

"You don't know?" Barsh asked. "Halls of the Dead are notoriously known to be places of enchantment. Places where grindels—like your spear—are used to reanimate bodies of those long gone."

Jilo snorted. "That sounds like children's tales."

"Barsh knows not what it is," Barsh said. "But Barsh knows that everything comes at a cost. And this spear is no different." He turned his head down and mumbled something to himself.

"What was that?" Jilo asked, leaning closer to the odd Burrower.

"Barsh cannot say," Barsh said, keeping his face down.

Scov reached across the table and seized the Burrower by the tufts of the shoulder.

"Agh!" Barsh cried.

"Tell us, Barsh," Scov growled.

"The spear!" Barsh exclaimed. "Barsh thinks he knows that spear! Let Barsh go!"

Scov dropped him reactively, eyes wide. "Know it?"

Barsh nodded. "First job, when Barsh left the Hidden Forest …" He paused, breathless, as Jilo began to put the pieces together in his mind.

"You betrayed us that night?" Jilo hissed. "You are the one who tipped off Therador to the Great Hunt? You rotten waste, you—"

Jilo had reared up by this point, but Scov blocked him with an arm. "Is this true, Barsh? Did you really send Therador to the Greenwood to retrieve the spear?"

It took a moment, but then Barsh moaned. "For a lotta gold!"

Scov nodded. "Well then, traitor—"

"*Don't* call Barsh a traitor, Nestler!" Barsh snapped.

"If you insist on not being called a traitor, then there is only one thing left for you to do. Help us get Ka-Del back!"

"For what coin?" Barsh asked. Jilo was going to wring his neck if he mentioned money again.

"For enough coin! Coin and honour, you pathetic fool!" Scov slammed back his drink and looked Barsh dead in the eyes, his own fiery with purpose.

"If we leave Therador with the spear, we risk losing the war. Their knowledge grows great, but it is clearly not great enough. What if Ka-Del allows them to advance their knowledge of Luminosity beyond what anybody on Q'ara can anticipate?" Scov asked. "We must bring it back into Jilo's hands. It is the only way."

"Fine," Barsh said, slamming his drink back. "But don't say Barsh didn't warn you." He stood, brushing himself down before hopping past Jilo and Scov. "What are you waiting for? Don't waste Barsh's time!"

---

The Hall of the Dead loomed over the city's nightscape like Death himself, shaped with a dominant arch at the highest point of the building, a hood covering an empty face. Behind it, the moon cowered betwixt scattered clouds.

Jilo knelt behind the lip of a nearby rooftop with the two Hidden Ones by his side, assessing the building and monitoring for Priests of Dirt. "Why are they here?" he whispered. "Why now?"

"They are preparing for something great," Scov replied. "Do not doubt this empire's power, Cousin. They have sought to own

Q'ara ever since they came here. And every year, it seems they take several hundred steps closer to their goal."

Memories flashed through Jilo's mind of the night Therador had hunted down Ka-Del and taken it from him. *"Take the grindel!"* their captain had yelled. *"Leave the boy. He'll freeze in these woods before morning comes."*

Therador had wanted the grindel—Ka-Del—for their own purposes, and yet it was only now, years later, that Jilo realised how much they still needed it. It seemed that whatever secrets Ka-Del held were still hidden from the Empire. And his mother …

He felt his stomach turn. He couldn't believe his mother was alive, let alone working for the enemy. He shared blood with her, and she shared blood with *them*. What did that make him?

"When we get in, Jilo," Barsh began, "you must find the spear."

Jilo shot Barsh a face full of daggers. "I will find it, and only *I* will hold it, understand?"

Barsh grunted in acknowledgement. "We can hold the rest of them back, no matter how great their number. Piatic local law enforcement could be present, too."

"What if your mother has Ka-Del, Cousin?" Scov asked.

"I don't care who has it, Scov," Jilo replied. "It's mine, and mine alone."

"But what if—"

"Then I'll end her!" Jilo hissed. "I'll seal the memory of her away. I'll lock her betrayals up with her broken body." His voice broke and he wrenched his gaze away from the two Hidden Ones.

Just then, a carriage stopped before the Hall and turned through gates that clanked as they were opened from behind. Mother. Jilo narrowed his eyes as he peered at it. Wherever she'd been, whatever she'd been up to, didn't matter. If they wanted Ka-Del, they needed to act.

"That's her," he said, pointing at the carriage as it disappeared beyond the gates. "What do we need to know about these Priests of Dirt, Barsh? Who are they beneath their masks?"

Barsh chuckled in a low, gravelly tone. "The Priests of Dirt are said to be the backbone of the Empire, acting as the head of the church that Therador predicates itself upon. The Church of Dirt believes in one idea: work. Work as hard as you can, because that's why you were put on this earth in the first place. Remember that when you die, you'll go back to it. And if you do not work" – he gulped – "be prepared to go back to the dirt *alive*."

"Alive?" Scov asked.

Barsh nodded. "If you are not prepared to commit your life to others and share in the labour, then you will be put back into the ground, alive or not. They call this *reclamation*. A word that allows them to justify the death of others."

"But, how—" Jilo began.

"Don't ask!" Barsh snapped. "Barsh has seen it happen once, and Barsh never wishes to see it again."

Jilo felt his neck crawl. "So they'll all be on highest alert?"

"They are *always* on highest alert. You know their masks?"

Jilo nodded, nervous.

"The front of a skull, sometimes human, sometimes not, fused to the horns or antlers of the hunted, a sign of their commitment to working for survival. Every skull you see them wear on their face belonged to someone who was put back into the ground once. Someone who did not do enough."

The quiet settled on them, but Barsh did not let it linger for long. "Let's go. In the front is a lobby that is closed off from the main hall. We can fight our way through whoever lies in there and then work out what to do next."

The group scampered down the building and crossed the road, keeping well away from the glimmer of the lamplight in the street. When they got to the front of the hall, Barsh pulled them to the side of the entry stairs. "Listen carefully," he whispered. "Barsh knows Piat nearly as well as Barsh's own burrows. Priests of Dirt are not common in these parts, and if they're here to find the spear, they won't be muckin' about. There's bound to be a lot of them, and they will stop at nothing short of achieving their goal. If they want this spear, Jilo, then we have two options: survive or be killed."

Jilo studied the Burrower.

"Bah!" Barsh scowled. "Let's be done with it, then! You head for the main hall, and Scov and Barsh will remove any of the immediate … impediments that stand in our way."

They moved up the stairs, using the stone pillars that ran down each side as cover. At the top, Barsh creaked open the massive door to the hall, jamming himself in the gap to keep it from clanking shut. He gestured for the other two to run past him. The way was clear. Ahead of them, in the foyer, was another set of doors made of frosted glass. The haze of shadows beyond it told Jilo they would not be alone; several people were roaming the main hall, and it was likely they were all Priests of Dirt. If he wanted to get to his mother and Ka-Del, he would need to fight. He steeled himself and inhaled slowly. "There's no time like the present," he whispered, and Scov nodded with him.

Barsh threw a holster filled with darts at Scov. "Let's use these, see if we can't take them down before they get to Jilo." The Burrower narrowed his gaze at Jilo. "Before we go in ... How much are you paying Barsh for his services?"

Jilo looked at the Burrower incredulously. "Are you serious?"

"Cousin Jilo will pay in multitudes," Scov growled.

Barsh nodded. "Well then, here's to not dying." He kicked the foyer doors open, and several priests turned to look in the trio's direction. "We're here for your spear!" Barsh yelled. The Priests of Dirt looked at each other, confused. "Not the ones in your pants, but if we need to, we'll take those too. Let's get 'em!"

The Burrower ran at the nearest priest, slamming his tiny feet into the cloaked body and pinning his opponent to the floor. Everyone watched in horror as Barsh ripped his Izog across the priest's neck so quickly, the man didn't even have time to scream. Then, the room exploded into a frenzy of cries. Blades were being unsheathed and there was chaos as men ran wildly towards the doors.

Jilo ran the circumference of the hall, noticing the many entrances and exits to other places in the building. He tried to think, searching for Ka-Del, listening for its hum. He heard its song of warning, of what was to come and what had come. A song of belonging. And it sang to *him*. He followed his instincts, darting down a thin alley between floor-to-ceiling bookshelves, opposite a wall of entombed bodies. Ka-Del was *here*. He knew it. The fire in his gut told him it was close, and it was in the wrong hands.

Ahead of him, a number of priests managed to thwart him from passing through the walkway, and he ran back the other way, in the direction of another few men waiting for him to return to the main hall.

They didn't attack. Instead, they held their swords out in front of them, staving him off. He stood still as the priests behind him closed the gap. Then, the men he stood before allowed in an illustrious figure in a deep blue dress who was holding the spear that mimicked its colour.

"This is not your fight, little yam," Jilo's mother, Talei, said. "If you turn and leave now, I will spare you and your weasel friends."

Ka-Del hummed, dulling his senses. It did not wish to go with her.

"So be it," was all she said.

# THEN
## *1888 AS*

Jilo limped away from the soft grass clearing as the afternoon sun set over his back, warming his wounds and bruises. These weasels could fight. He'd never felt so sore in all his life. He'd sparred with his father and uncles and cousins all the time in Sai-Kathan, but against the Nestlers and their Izog knives, he was overcome. He never thought he'd be bested by creatures less than half his height, armed with a pair of butter knives.

"Cousin Jilo!" Scov mourned. "Come back! Just once more, Scov promises!"

Jilo shook his head, turning to look back at his friend. "Seriously? I'm sick of being pummelled into the ground."

From behind Scov, Yva, his promised one, and her brothers Storc, Bisk, and Vril cackled upon the ground. Jilo scowled.

"That's enough for today, I think!" He began to walk away, despondent.

"Sparring is important, Cousin Jilo," panted Scov as he ran up to him, holding out Jilo's wooden staff, which was sharpened on one end to simulate a spear. Not only was he familiar with the weapons, but so were the Hidden Ones; on hunting expeditions, they were commonplace. He took it from his friend, feeling the smooth wood and the rope that was ornately tied around its centre as a makeshift grip.

"I know it's important." He sighed. "I'm just not patient enough to see myself improve against you. You're so much faster than me, both on your feet and in your mind."

"Excuses, Cousin Jilo," Scov replied, shrugging. "You are capable of anything. Look at how you came to be with us. There wasn't a moment you were certain you would survive."

It was true. Jilo grimaced at the memory of the past year. A lot had changed in that time, perhaps him most of all. Because life had given him a second chance, he'd felt the need to honour it. His father, on the other hand, did not share in his thinking and sat most days in the hut, rotting away on tabac-leaf smoke and sapwine, stuck in a cycle of remembering the end of his people.

*When we remember, we only receive a version of the other times we've remembered it, little yam,* his mother had always told him. *We can never relive the same things. We aren't made perfectly enough for that.*

If only Hiro would heed these seeds of wisdom that Talei had left them with before she'd died in the flood.

Jilo tsk-d, returning his gaze to Scov. "All right. One more time, Scov. But then, I need some food."

---

The Greenwood of the Hidden Forest was the lush centre from which all life seemed to travel from. Every night after helping the Nestlers with various errands, sparring, or cooking, Jilo would sit back in his hut and marvel at the mystique and beauty of nature. It reminded him in some ways of Sai-Kathan, though it felt like the denser forestry that his old tribe had bordered on rather than the tribal land itself. Verdant green pan-din trees and greatferns, ancient relatives to the Great Trees that had once dominated Q'ara, climbed to the sky, where stars hung in bright arrangements upon a boundless deep blue.

Jilo and Hiro's hut was a small, thatched thing, created with the help of the Nestlers when they'd first arrived in the Greenwood a year ago. It wasn't dissimilar from their old home, but the past year had given them plenty of time to make it more like they remembered. Two chambers for sleeping and a central, open-air space for a fire was all that it took to make the hut feel cosy.

Here, everyone lived in close quarters, the grounds of the wood lined with dozens of huts, grown over by ferns and bushes but neatly kept, trim and proper. Maintenance was important, and the Nestlers took to pruning back the forestry around their homes to create the shape of streets and the impression of a miniature town.

At night, everything in the forest was coated in a glowing radiance, like a moon shadow, but of greens, blues, and purples instead of simple white light. Luminosity, the Nestlers called it. A sign of old magic that still ran in the veins of the earth today. Jilo had still not recovered from the awe he'd felt on the first night he'd slept here under the stars. It made the forest less sinister and more welcoming.

Tonight, however, the feeling was held back by the lack of his father's presence. Jilo had grown used to Hiro's annoying ability to drift around like stale air, his breath ripe with the burn of spirits and his mind diminished by grief. His father's pride would be the death of him. Jilo knew this well. Though he resented the way that Hiro would usually slink back into the hut, fearful of the world outside that had taken everything from him, he also worried that his father was not home now. Jilo had chosen to face what he'd been met with that fateful night one year ago, when the very thing that sustained humanity had turned on his people. Maybe it just took Hiro that long to make the same choice.

He left the hut, heading to a central fire where many of his friends were sitting, roasting duck and drinking sapwater, a light and sweet unfermented version of what his father drank too much of. "Cousins." He nodded to the Nestlers about the fire. Scov and Yva waved at him. Behind them sat Garv the elder and Clev, Scov's uncle and another of the elders of the Greenwood.

"Ah, young Jilo," Clev said. "Care for some food? We have plenty to share."

Jilo nodded as he sat, his stomach rumbling. He realised he hadn't eaten since before the afternoon sparring session, and he was famished. "Have you seen my father, elders?"

Clev shook his head. "Cavtil called in earlier today to gather him for a meeting ahead of the Great Hunt. He hasn't been there for much of the day."

Jilo's ears pricked up. "Much of the day? That is unlike Father." He stood. "I'll eat later, Clev, I—"

"Child," Clev said, shaking his head. "Clev thinks you should leave your father to himself. This is a great moment of stepping forward out of the darkness. Heavens above only know how long Hiro has harboured this grief for. Anything he can do to reconnect with the land and feel what he must in his heart to return to us, he must do alone. Do you understand?"

Though Jilo felt a sense of worry at the thought of staying here and eating merrily, he nodded. If the wisdom of these people had taught him anything in the last year, it was that the hardest parts of the journey, when overcome alone, bore the most fruit.

"One who has the strength to conquer their enemies is strong. Stronger than most." Garv took a sip of his drink. "But one who has the strength to conquer themselves is mightier than all." He glared over his drink at Jilo, his beady, black eyes capturing Jilo's attention like deep wells. "Now sit, boy, and eat with us."

Jilo sat cross-legged by the fire, next to Yva. He loved her like a sister. Time had deadened the reaction he'd once had to being in conversation with talking weasels. These creatures were a family. *His* family.

As he reached out to grab a piece of meat from the trestle that hung above the fire, Yva placed a soft paw on his arm. "Yva knows it is hard to relax when a loved one is enduring the worst." She smiled at him. "But you need to be your best self for them, Cousin."

Jilo felt a tug of tears at the edges of his eyes. "I just want him to be okay," he choked out. He'd remembered the feeling, the immense weight of relief, like a warm blanket, of seeing his father alive after the flood. Though Hiro had feigned indifference, his wall of stoicism forever unbroken, Jilo knew he'd felt the same way. Twin souls lost in tragedy. All they had these days was each other. The Nestlers filled in the gaps to the best of their ability, but it would never be the same as it had been when Jilo was a boy. When he'd been able to go to his mother and help her sew garments, or walk with his father through the forests of Sai-Kathan, gathering food with the rest of their people.

Feeling tired, Jilo soon left the Nestlers where he had found them, and resigned himself to his tent. Of course, it was empty when he got there, so he got into bed, and pressed his eyes shut in an attempt at forgetting. Hiro would return when *he* wanted to, and nothing Jilo could do would change that.

Jilo couldn't sleep. The sun set unusually late this far north, and the spring days were longer now. The moment the darkness had made its overture known, Jilo had fallen into his bed, a kind of vine-wound hammock, determined to rest. His stamina from constant sparring was depleted, and yet his usual ability to sleep without interruption would be stalled by another anxiety. Because Hiro had still not returned.

His father was out there somewhere, in the Greenwood.

"La!" he yelled, his anger blinding. How dare his father do this to him? Leave without nary a note or message. What if Hiro was lost, wandering aimlessly? His head was not right, he could've—

*Sapwine.* Jilo hated the stuff. He'd sworn off drink already, and he wasn't even an adult yet. He bet that's what had happened: Hiro had gone off, flask in hand, and gotten lost. It wasn't cold outside, but it was chilly enough that it wouldn't be a comfortable sleep out in the Greenwood.

Jilo exited the hut with frustrated vigour, taking his wooden shaft with him in case he'd come across any wildlife. Though they were otherwise fairly safe, the risk of running into pythons and hyo cats was high at this time of year. He collected some rainwater in a flask from the outdoor chamber by the hut and swung his blanket over his shoulder. If he couldn't find Hiro, he'd have to get some sleep somewhere.

He wandered for a time, using the Luminous plants and fungi around him to find his way through the dark alcoves of palms and ferns. The loudest sound in the night were his footsteps. Trudging through fertile ground, pale green on the cusp of drying in the coming season, Jilo felt his mind clear with each step. Out here, he could let go of what had been troubling him. He chuckled. Clev was right. That's why his father was out here, too. How little he'd trusted Hiro all these months since the flood. Jilo had good reason to feel so resentful towards his father. Hiro had been the strongest man in the tribe, and yet here he was in the Greenwood, crippled by the past. No matter how hard Jilo tried, he just couldn't understand it. *Pick yourself up and move on, old man,* he thought. *That's what I did.*

The gentle ripple of water rang out from up ahead, the sound equivalent to the sharpening of a blade. He knew where he was. This was his thinking spot. The lake of the Greenwood was an uninhibited place, known for its clean water catchment in the rainy months. In the warmer months though, it went untouched, making it the perfect place for Jilo to sit whenever he needed a moment to himself.

The glow of Luminosity in the forest around him was only offset by one other thing, which outshone the rest of the plantlife. Ka-Del's spearhead was pressed into the earth, and before it was a great black lump, a motionless void of shadow. Though it was dark, he knew that outline. Father. Relief bore down on him and he couldn't hold back his smile.

"Father!" he called, stepping closer to the bearer of the spear. "Father, I found you!"

No reply came. Drunk again, no doubt. Hiro had probably spent most of his tears alone out here in the woods. Jilo would walk home with him in the inevitable silence that had grown between them, and tomorrow would be like any other day. He stepped closer, one foot after the other, watching his father's shape remain still in the darkness. "Father?" he whispered, tapping his father's unresponsive shoulder. His breath caught, and he shoved Hiro, harder this time.

Tomorrow would not be like any other day.

Hiro's body slumped forward, and Jilo choked as he realised what had happened. His father's body was sliding down Ka-Del's shaft towards the spearhead that was buried in the soil. Honour bound, all Kathani were to die by their own sword when they had nothing left to give.

But cowardice had bound Hiro. Cowardice alone.

Jilo screamed, his inarticulate gargles strangling the forest around him as he charged at his father's body, the shell of what had once been a great man. It was coated in sticky blood as the spear came undone from the ground and the whole mass crashed into the dirt. An eruption of vomit burned its way out of Jilo's mouth at the sight of the thick and unctuous blood. He wiped his mouth, coughing as his eyes began to sting.

"How *dare* you?" Jilo sobbed, tears streaming down his face and blurring his vision. "How *dare* you *leave me?*"

Hiro had ended it all upon his blade, the very heirloom that had marked him as a leader of his people. All because of a transitory pain that would go away, or pretend to, in time. Mother would've hidden her pain well. It struck him as he cried that of both his parents, it was the one who had perished first that would have never let go.

Resentment spewed forward. How could his father have done this? What was the life he'd lived, that it was so different from his own son's?

Mother's voice crooned to him in the night as Jilo fell to his knees, a sobbing and wretched mess. *We create our reality, little yam. If we can create that, then we can dream of anything we want.*

# NOW

## *2055 AS*

"**W**HY ARE YOU DOING this?" Jilo demanded of his mother amidst the crowd of priests. In the background, Scov and Barsh were back to back, Izogs guarding one another as they stood in the centre of a crowd of priests, oblivious to his situation.

"My son, the way forward is through the pursuit of knowledge," his mother replied, sincerity dripping from her voice. This was not the woman who'd raised him. The countless years since he'd last seen her had changed her for the worse.

"And you choose the way forward with Therador's hands around your neck?" Jilo demanded. "There are better ways toward progress, Mother. We create our reality. That's what you always told me." He watched as a flash of recognition passed over her face. She remembered those words. And yet, it seemed like they no longer defined her. She had a new mantra now. Progress in the face of whatever challenges you. Stop at nothing. Find *more*.

"*This* is our reality, Jilo," his mother replied, gesturing around. "This empire came here to escape its past nearly two thousand years ago, and still we struggle to survive on the land that we first settled on."

Jilo laughed. "You expect me to believe that? I don't know how much of your blood is Theradoran, but I know some of it belongs to my people, *our* people. The Kathani were the first humans to come to Q'ara, Mother, despite what your hubris allows you to believe. We chose a better life. One where the Aobians and the Hidden Ones remained untouched, and peace was our point of connection with the land and its people. The Sickness might have eradicated that tradition, but *you* chose to abandon it. You chose to abandon me *and* Father."

His mother's eyes grew wet, though she blinked back the tears. "Don't lure me from my path, boy. Your father chose his fate. And you've chosen yours." The priests closed in around him, blades extended towards him. They were so close that if he moved a muscle, he would catch some part of his skin on steel.

"Why Ka-Del?" Jilo asked, stalling.

"Because," Talei began, "Ka-Del is one of many answers to the secrets of this land. It may even be the answer to the Sickness. It is cut from the wood of a Great Tree, long since fallen."

Jilo's frown increased. The Sickness. Ka-Del held answers to the thing that had single-handedly killed his people and ruined his life?

At that moment, a tiny dart sputtered through her arm, re-emerging in the direction of Jilo himself, and he moved out of the way as his mother crashed to the floor.

Talei wailed, clinging onto her wounded arm and dropping Ka-Del. The priests scattered. The rattle of the spear redirected everyone's attention to it, and Jilo leapt as Barsh ran past, connecting a hefty paw with the underside of a snarling priest's chin. Scov bolted at full speed up the stone wall to their right, tossing darts from the satchel Barsh had given him to keep the priests suppressed in fear as Jilo collected Ka-Del and headed for the broken door that had been barricaded moments before.

A shadow slipped across the doorway, giving way to a different sort of priest who appeared before Jilo, stopping him in his tracks. This one's appearance was the most threatening, judging by the mask he wore and the necklace of angular, messy human teeth about his neck. His arms were painted entirely in black, and the mask was tiny, forced to adhere to his head unnaturally. Jilo felt nauseous at the sight of it. Had this once belonged to a child?

Jilo barely considered it before the priest produced a long fork with three spokes, shoving it forward. He tried to slip beneath it but his feet came out from under him and he crept slowly back across the floor on his palms, looking up at the menacing weapon. In the commotion he'd dropped Ka-Del again, and now he was so pinned down he couldn't wriggle over to it if he tried.

"Nalor!" Jilo's mother cried from behind them. "The spear! Take the spear!"

"Yes, Mother." The deep voice from behind the mask rolled like thunder. He pushed his fork forward even more so that the cool metal touched Jilo's throat. "Do not move, worm, or I'll part your head from your neck."

"Mother?" Jilo gulped.

"You don't know?" the priest hissed. "I am also her spawn. There isn't room in this world for two of us, blood kin, and I will not go back to the dirt. One of us must."

Jilo felt the sounds of fighting, the echo of steel on steel across the chamber, begin to soften as his heartbeat rose to his temples. She had another family?

His mother cackled, a sound unlike any he had ever heard. She'd appeared beside them, picking up Ka-Del for what felt like the hundredth time. It glowed and it hummed, and Jilo knew it was trying to show her something. An image of the past or a warning of what was to come. Then, she closed her eyes, standing beside the priest called Nalor, and sucked in a breath. The light of Ka-Del moved through her and she exhaled slowly, opening her eyes, which appeared bluer than they ever had. It was as though Ka-Del and his mother were both glowing so brightly, they were becoming one. He'd seen something similar before, when his father had carried the spear. The night the Sickness came, Father's arm had been blue to the elbow and alight. This, however, was more extreme: as though his mother had lost her human aspect and stood before him as an extension of the strange weapon.

"It ... heals!" she cried, and Jilo watched with wide eyes as her torn skin from one of Scov's darts knitted itself closed like it was conducted by some invisible surgeon to do so.

Then, she gasped, and her features became blurry in the enveloping light, like a shadow's outline, only she was filled with light. "Mother, let go!" Jilo screamed. Confusion tore at him, caught between the reality of her betrayal and the fact that she was his only parent.

"No! You will not break the connection!" Nalor yelled, launching a leather boot into Jilo's face and knocking him back to the ground. Jilo moaned in pain, instinctively clamping his bleeding nose with his hands.

The light of Ka-Del had grown greater than itself and Jilo's mother now, and he felt obligated to watch as it drowned out all the other details of the hall. In the back, Scov and Barsh moved silently in battle with the other priests, and yet the light continued to grow, swallowing all signs that they'd ever been there. Jilo squinted through the blazing blue radiance as it grew hot as flame. His mother was crying, a mixture of victory and terror painted across her expression.

The next several moments were stitched together like they were one. Barsh swinging out of the dense blue glow and taking Nalor's fork as another blade scraped past the Burrower's neck. Scov planting a firm foot into the priest's mask as he was gripped by two other priests and tossed aside. Barsh fixing the man in place, catching his arm in between spokes of the fork as he drove it into the wall.

Jilo could do nothing for them now. His mother was becoming nearly a flicker of what she had been before, no longer human but somehow assembled into the light Ka-Del continued to produce. She was receding into the air itself, fading away like a spirit. The light was consuming her, and her sobbing became a shrill, agonised wail. Jilo's heart thumped with desperation, struggling against the cage of his innards to be with hers. He couldn't let this happen.

He had to venture in, had to keep something of his alive ... But did she deserve it? He reached up to where the blurred visage of what had once been her arm clung to Ka-Del and pulled on the spear. She didn't deserve it. Not this ending. She'd made mistakes, but she was still his mother. But then, another voice entered his mind, the words of Ne-Lo the visionary, quoted by his father: *Be aware that idols are always hidden in those you love.*

"Sing to *me*, Ka-Del," he said, desperation urging him to speak again. "Sing to *me*!"

Ka-Del did not sing. It screamed like it had been pierced in the place where its heart lay, like it couldn't bear to see that what it had warned would come to fruition. Jilo gripped the handle and felt the world slow before reality split into a series of moments. Blue light rushed up his arm, connecting him to his mother's fate.

The first one to wield Ka-Del had been Ne-Lo the Visionary, a sage that supposedly had been able to read the future via the spear. Unbelievably, Jilo felt a kinship with the legendary figure as all the paths of time, every possibility, lay before him and filled his mind. Every possibility, where they went and where they came from, was within his grasp because of *the spear*. Jilo was a visionary, and the blue light rendered unto him indicated that out of all the paths he could see, none would end well.

Suddenly, the paths of the future were replaced with events of the past. The Sickness of the river played back before him, and his irrational fear of water forced him to look away. His home in the Greenwood, his father dying, the spear taken from him ... and behind those moments, the brewing of a war, the declaration of assault on Q'ara from the Theradoran emperor. But when he looked ahead, he saw one thing that gave him hope, buried in a moment of catastrophe.

Ka-Del knew. It knew *all*. This war would end, and peace would come again. But not without the death of his mother. Somehow, seeing the moment that Ka-Del overwhelmed her and caused her to fall to her death played before him softened the blow of what he knew was coming. It made it all okay, gave it a purpose, and helped him carry the weight of another parent, dead.

He ripped Ka-Del from his mother's frozen grip, and time retracted like a band of tarpaulin stretched too thin. Sound, motion, and atmosphere came back to him, and there they were, amidst the combat taken up with the Priests of Dirt. Nalor looked at him, shocked, as Jilo ran back from him and their mother fell to the ground, all the light of the spear leaving her. Fallen down she seemed ... ordinary. But she was not dead, like Ka-Del had shown him.

That's when Jilo realised he was already too late to change what would happen next.

Ka-Del was to be the victim this night.

He slammed the handle of the spear into Nalor, sending the priest to the hard tiled floor. Nalor gasped to get the wind back that had left his lungs, but he was stuck where he was, giving Jilo time to channel Ka-Del's song, feel its warmth, let the dark blue light flow through him. He had never let the spear take this much command before, but he knew that this would be the only way. On one side of the room, Scov was being held against the wall, an elbow the width of his torso pressed against his throat. Barsh was on the ground, a number of priests on top of him in a mess of black robes, silver flashes, and skull masks. They would die if Jilo—and Ka-Del—didn't act *now*.

The spear's song grew even more intense, so much so that Jilo felt a burning sensation rush through his limbs, from his fingers to his chest. It was like he'd become a one-way valve for the power it contained, and it had nowhere to go but back—back to Ka-Del's head. *Sing to me,* he thought. *Sing, Ka-Del, one more time.*

The light concentrated in the spearhead and the metal grew white-hot, exploding with a build-up of energy. Fire roared through the room, bouncing off the stone walls and cracking the tiles on the floor. Jilo let go of the spear handle, acutely aware of the danger it posed to hold on. He'd saved Ka-Del once, reclaiming it from the ruined body of his father. But now, Ka-Del was saving him.

The room filled with light so bright that he could no longer see, bodies crashing into his sides as he rolled on the floor, keeping his eyes squeezed shut. He thought he could hear his mother's screams and Scov calling his name before a sound of shattering like the breaking of a thousand glass bottles filled his ears and the room went dark. Lanterns once lit were now smoking plumes, and masses of black robes lay scattered about the room, motionless.

Jilo felt a furry paw grab his collar and he got to his feet, coughing through clouds of dust. Broken tiles impeded his movement and he squinted through the aftermath, trying to see the door to the foyer of the hall. "Good earth. Get up, Cousin Jilo!" It was Scov. Barsh shoved them forward. "Go, go, go! Before the rest of them come!"

As they clambered towards the door, Jilo noticed bits of glimmering metal and wooden splinters all over the floor, spread far and wide. Ka-Del's remnants. The spear had sacrificed itself for the sake of the war effort and to save Jilo. Had it been cognisant? Had it possessed an awareness of the role it had played and the power it'd had?

Jilo snatched a shard of metal from beside him as he ran past, holding onto a piece of what had been his father's spear and his father's before him. Jilo, Scov, and Barsh burst through the foyer doors, past a series of priests who were flocking into the building from the outside, and out onto the street.

"Cart! Over there!" cried Barsh. "Jump in the back!"

A horse-drawn cart moved down the road, wheels rattling on the cobblestones of Piat. Barsh leapt into the air, seizing the reins and planting both feet firmly onto the chest of the unsuspecting driver. The horses screamed, but he slowed them to a halt as Jilo and Scov got into the cart attached to the back. Jilo pulled the canvas tarpaulin over their heads as Priests of Dirt made their way towards them. Jilo peered through the cart, able to glimpse the driver's bench from behind.

"Sorry, chum!" Barsh chuckled. "But you've gotta go!" Two paws gripped the collapsed driver by the collar and hauled him up. In moments, the sound of a body smacking the road accompanied the roll of cartwheels, and before Jilo knew it, Barsh was driving the horses away from the commotion outside the Hall of the Dead. They'd escaped with their lives.

Jilo wrapped the tiny piece of Ka-Del in some fabric from his shirt and clutched it in his hands. He would never let it go. As they rode away from the city centre into cool country air, the lamplight quickly fading to a more complete darkness, Jilo mourned the loss of Ka-Del, the only thing that had tethered him to his past life. Eventually, sleep came to his exhausted body as two questions lulled him into his dreamstate.

Had Ka-Del known that it had needed to be destroyed?

Did *all* the supposed 'grindels' need to be destroyed?

# THEN

## *1888 AS*

It had been weeks since his father's death, but Jilo still woke in the mornings, unsure of where Hiro was. The absent space in the hut was so noticeable that it stung to dwell there, and he'd recently resorted to sleeping on a spare hammock at Scov's home, which was further down the road that cut through the Nestler huts of the Greenwood.

Today, the first day of summer, marked the annual Great Hunt, a time in which the Nestlers and Burrowers of the Hidden Forest came together to find their first bounty of the year and celebrate their life given to them by their ancestors and the patronage they shared for the earth. In summer, at the peak of the lifecycle, the earth often gave back. The Nestler elders celebrated the end of the hunt at dawn, where a grand feast would be held with the winnings presented to the people to share. On the walls of the elders' tent hung the many frames of their catches over the years, from strong, overgrown bucks to fallen Greatbirds.

Jilo had come with Scov to the elders' tent, and they would hunt together as cousins later that night. He looked around the tent in awe as the Nestler elders gathered with the Burrower elders in a segregated room at the very back. This was the first time he'd seen the Nestler's underground relatives, and he was still getting used to the sight of them. They had much more scruffy fur than the Nestlers and stood nearly a head taller than them. They also had cream-coloured bellies, something that some Nestlers had but was not a mark of the general populace. Lastly, their eyes were fuller and reflected light. These Hidden Ones were clearly built for the dark, as was signified by their lives underneath the Greenwood, where they lived in complex tunnel systems. Today, however, they emerged to help the Nestlers catch their greatest prizes.

Emerging from the meeting room first was Clev, Scov's uncle and elder. "Jilo." He nodded in greeting. "Before you hunt with us, you have much to learn. We do not hunt like humans."

Garv, one of the other Nestler elders, appeared beside him. "Yes, much to learn," he added. "Come, child. Before you can take anything from this earth, you must see it for what it truly is. You must see *yourself* for what you truly are, too. One does not go without the other."

With that, Clev and Garv walked away, and Jilo noted the seriousness in Scov's eyes. "What now?"

"Now, Cousin," Scov began, "you learn."

Scov led Jilo from the tent, out past the main road, and deeper into the Greenwood. Jilo felt sick retracing these steps. They were nearly the same as those he'd taken when he'd found his father. Reflexively, he clutched Ka-Del, peering at its handle. It was shining green. Perhaps today, only good things lay ahead.

Eventually, they came to a clearing that buffeted the River Tomei's northwestern channel. The thing that had killed his people ran right behind them. He hadn't heard the rush of this river in a long time, and the trauma of its stillness, its unpredictable nature, caused a lump to rise in his throat. It was the reason his father was dead and the reason *he* was here. Why had the Sickness never caused problems this far north?

In the clearing, Yva stood with her mother and Nestler elder Zya, looking solemn. Behind them, Cavtil, Clev, and Garv lingered with knives in hand. Real weapons. There would be no sparring session coming, Jilo feared.

"Good morning, Jilo," Cavtil said. The little elder was more serious than usual. Cavtil had been a comfort to Jilo in the days since his father's passing, but now his tone was cold and commanding. "The earth gave you life. In return, you must learn to respect it with every facet of your being. Every aspect of nature resides within our stewardship. That is what we strive for on Q'ara. Harmony."

"You wish to join the Great Hunt, human boy?" Zya asked next. Her voice was as sweet as Yva's, but there was no denying the years had wisened her.

"Yes, elder," Jilo replied.

"Then you must understand how we give and take from the earth. If we do not partake fairly, we go back to the ground where we belong." The words rang in his head. *Go back to the ground.*

The Hidden Ones had always been careful in the ways they went about harvesting and hunting. Their lives worked in tandem with nature, much like Jilo's people had. Whatever they harvested, for example, they allowed to grow back, or even encouraged. If they did any wrong to the land, or the people in it, their punishments were severe, but almost always entirely just. He knew how this was going to go. Tonight, he would be invited along to hunt with them. He was one of *their* people now.

"To hunt means to meet nature with respect for the life it offers us." Garv's lecturing tone stirred Jilo from his thoughts. "But, Child Jilo, you have seen firsthand the worst form of disrespect for life and we will not allow you to repeat it, no matter the darkness that may grow in your heart."

Father. They dared to declare his own father a betrayer of nature? He'd led his people like his father had before him, in the great traditions of the Kathani, maintaining the land perfectly. He'd rationed meats as necessary and grown edible plants and vegetables. Now he was dead. But that was no betrayal. That was a sickness of the mind. Jilo felt his blood boil, and Ka-Del throbbed in his hand.

"My father loved the e-earth." He choked on the last word.

"That may be so, Child Jilo," Garv replied. "But he went back to it before it wished to reclaim him. That was not his right."

"His right?" Jilo cried through fresh tears. "He had no *right* to choose death? How can you say that?"

"Cousin," Scov said, reaching out to touch Jilo's arm. "This is a lesson in our beliefs—"

"I will not adhere to your beliefs so simply, *Cousin!*" Jilo scolded. "Your people took my father and I in. But we *lost* our people. We lost *all* of them. You will never know how that feels. My father ... He had nothing left. He was the tribe leader, like all of *you* are to the Nestlers." Jilo gestured to each of the elders. "If you felt you had failed your people, would you not feel worthless?"

"Your father was an honourable man, Jilo," Cavtil said. "You mistake us. He made a decision to die, but he did not *choose* to die. Not with a mind so clouded as his."

Jilo fell to his knees, dropping Ka-Del. Its green glimmer went out as he let go of it, but he didn't care. He heaved and moaned, his voice thick with grief. He would not accept his father's death as a denial of nature's rule. Did the Nestlers not understand that Hiro had been a broken man? And now, the people around him, who had looked after him, taken him in and treated him like one of their own, simply stood there and *watched* him break. He would have no choice but to participate in whatever trial they had planned. But he couldn't slow the tears pooling at his feet until the next words were spoken.

"Jilo, son of Hiro," announced Zya, ignoring his outburst. "You are here today to commit yourself to your father's honour. To continue his legacy and carve a new path for your lineage. You are here as the first human to take part in the Great Hunt.

You are here to understand your responsibilities as a dweller on this land of Q'ara, as a human ... and as a Nestler. Can you do this? Are you strong enough to accept this challenge, Jilo, son of Hiro?"

Jilo sniffed, glaring at the elder through a curtain of tears.

"I ... am strong enough."

"Very well," Zya replied. "Then, the earth takes back what it is owed."

"The earth takes back what it is owed!" cried Clev.

"The earth takes back what it is owed!" bellowed the rest of the Nestlers, jumping into action. Jilo grabbed Ka-Del from the dew-soaked grass and stood, readying himself. He parried the way the Nestlers had taught him, with a focus on his hips in relation to the spear. He kept his wrists loose to manage the weight of the spear as it came to strike against the Nestlers' tiny Izog knives. Within the first few moments of combat, he fended off Yva and Scov before dropping Clev to his knees, the shaft of the spear prodding the Nestler's neck so that he could not move to his feet.

As soon as those three were out of the way, Zya, Garv, and Cavtil posed the greatest threat. They stood in formation, like a wall, and each had the ability to spin their knives in their hands so fast they looked like whirring dragonflies in the sunlight. They marched closer to Jilo, moving him around the clearing. He could only walk backwards. He had to think of a way to disrupt their formation quickly or—

Zya leapt onto him, her tiny feet crossed around his neck. He crashed to the ground, the impact causing the air to leave his lungs as the elder kept him pinned down. Cavtil pocketed his knives before holding Jilo's ankles, and Garv tossed his weapons on the ground and twirled his whiskers. "Well, Child Jilo," he rumbled, "you are honourable. You know when to keep going and when to concede. With those two decisions in balance, you'll satisfy the cravings of the earth for years to come." He gestured at Cavtil and Zya to step away from Jilo and held out a paw to help him up from the ground. "Your father would be proud."

The tears streamed from Jilo's eyes, briny liquid stinging on the way out, and he felt the summation of weeks' worth of grief explode from within. In his hand, Ka-Del glowed green, and the feeling of the gnarled wooden handle felt oddly warming to him. The spear, he realised, never let him feel alone. Perhaps, the spirit of his father dwelled on in it still.

The Nestlers gathered around the boy and comforted him with gentle paws and clinging hugs. "Tonight," Zya began, "we will commence the Great Hunt, and it will be our greatest honour to have you, child of the Greenwood, among our family. May the light go with you."

---

Three hours after sunset, those taking part in the Great Hunt disembarked from the central meeting point of the elders' tent.

Groups of Nestlers and Burrowers went their separate ways into the Greenwood with different plans and visions of what they might find in the night. Scov and Jilo were together for the night, and Scov's plan was simple: catch a deer of the Greenwood.

Jilo and Scov had gone a ways out into the forest so that they could no longer see the glow of the Nestler settlement. They waited in dense shrubbery and swore to intermittent blocks of silence. It was counterintuitive, but each time some sound sprung from the woods, they would cease speaking, and when such a sound went away, both quickly realised just how unsettling it was to be lost in the dark of the forest. Conversation, even in whispers, was enough to make the venture bearable.

There was a hint of autumn in the Hidden Forest, and though many Luminous plants remained green and verdant, several others had reddened or were yellowing at the fringes. That meant food sources were less numerous, and if Scov's theory was correct, deer would be roaming during the night, looking to satiate their hunger.

There were two kinds of deer in the Hidden Forest, and of course Scov's ambition was to catch the more coveted one. The Greatdeer were Luminous creatures, influenced by the magic of the Hidden Forest. They stood twice the height of a regular deer, but, as was to be expected, were at least half as common to spot. Their sheer weight would be enough to pose a challenge for an entire team of Nestler hunters, so Jilo knew this plan would be no small feat for him and Scov.

The scuttle of something through the trees alerted Scov and Jilo after a period of total stillness. Jilo looked up through the leaves above his head and could see nothing, but Scov's Nestler eyes allowed him more vision. "Bah!" he exclaimed. "Other Nestlers disturbing our position!"

"Do you think they're on the trail of something?" Jilo asked.

"Scov does not know. But Scov recalls previous hunts, and most of the time, Hidden Ones find our greatest bounties around midnight."

Midnight? That meant there were still a few hours left that they would have to spend on the ground, their bellies pressed against the dirt.

More pattering feet above gave Jilo the chance to wriggle around a little and find temporary relief in a new position. But Scov's face only showed concern. "Lots of Nestlers moving above, Cousin Jilo," Scov said.

"Is that ... unusual?"

"Mmm, somewhat," Scov began, "but—"

Scuttling feet again. Voices whispering frantically. Something was not right.

And then, the faint smell of something Jilo had not smelled in quite some time reached his nostrils. Smoke.

Jilo tasted the smoke as Ka-Del's song came alive. He knew it well enough now, knew what to look for. The entire spear was a deep, dark blue, and he leant onto his side, smothering the signal for danger with his entire body. Without knowing what lay around the corner, he didn't want their position to be given away.

The sound of crackling came after that of heavy footsteps, and Scov went still, his ears pricked up. "No," he breathed. "There will be no fire in the Greenwood!"

"Smoke 'em out!" came a stranger's voice. The tiny clearing where Scov and Jilo were hidden was bushy enough that they might go unseen, but these strangers were holding torches in their hands. They were going to smoke out the Nestlers in the treetops.

A party of leather-clad men shuffled through the area in a V formation, each one with a sheathed blade by his side and a lit torch in hand. North of the Hidden Forest were the city of Piat and the Rocklands, a region to the southwest of Therador. But these men were not Piatic. They were from the Theradoran Empire, led by one particularly chilling figure at the head of their formation, a person draped in cloaks as dark as night. Their face was covered by a crudely-fashioned mask that looked like a real skull. Forced into the sides of the skull were long tusks from a boar or similar, like horns.

Jilo shivered as he felt Ka-Del pulse more rhythmically beneath him. It did not want them to be here. "Scov," he whispered. "Who is that?" He nodded to the person with the mask.

"Scov does not believe it," Scov replied. "That is a Priest of Dirt from the Empire of Therador. They do not show their faces, because they embody the message of mortality for all to observe.

Their belief is simple: if you come from the earth, you must work hard enough to sustain it."

"That doesn't sound so different from the belief of your people, Scov," Jilo replied, watching the men as they walked around, holding their torches up high enough to smoke the treetops.

"Our people, Cousin Jilo," Scov shot back. "But you are correct. The difference is in the execution of such beliefs. Scov will say no more, because Scov knows no more."

Scov's beady eyes watched the humans as they moved away from the area through a path between trees several feet away. "Now, cease your questions, Cousin. These men have been sent here for something. Good earth! They know we are on the Great Hunt. They know we are not confined to the Hidden Forest, where they cannot go. Let us pursue them." With that, Scov scampered away, his soft footpads barely moving the blades of grass that he danced upon as he took off in the direction the men had gone.

"Damn it!" Jilo scowled before getting to his feet. He had no choice. Scov was well on the way. Ka-Del grew bluer, a colour that Jilo recalled from the very night the Sickness had taken the people of Sai-Kathan. Whatever lay ahead of them was bad.

It proved fortuitous as Jilo ran through the trees, Scov's tiny figure barely outlined in the break-through moonlight between the canopies. A fair distance away, the smoke had evolved into plumage, spiralling through the treetops. The men had started a fire in the Greenwood. Given that it was the beginning of autumn, everything was mostly dry. Expectant. And ready to ignite.

Jilo knew well the mantra of the Hidden Ones when it came to fire. It was the antithesis of life. Everything they did, they did without fire. They cured their meats and ate their fruits fresh. They sustained the land around them until such a time that it burned of its own accord, and when it did, they managed it to the best of their abilities. But this? This was an act of malice.

Fire spat from a lit bush, its embers like speckled droplets of rain moving in the wrong direction. The embers formed pools of burning on higher leaves and branches, and before Jilo could perceive it, fire was running up tree trunks, out of control. He could do nothing to contain it.

As the trees lit like torches of the earth itself, the heat began to bite his skin, his clothes, and his mind. Smoke moved in billows now, occasionally becoming so thick he lost his orientation. But as he ran, he *just* managed to keep Scov's outline in his sights.

He got closer to Scov at the next turn that they made through the trees, only to see his tiny friend leap through the air, pouncing on the shoulders of none other than a Theradoran soldier. With the backdrop a drawn curtain of flame, the exact moments of attack disappeared into oblique silhouettes dancing on a background of orange, and Jilo found himself looking down at Ka-Del in his hand while his heart pounded in his chest. With all the orange hues of the Greenwood ablaze, Ka-Del still cut through it with its bare blue. *Danger. Mortal danger.*

Ka-Del's song was so loud it translated as words that swirled in Jilo's mind.

SAVE THEM, JILO.

GO NOW AND SAVE THEM!

BEFORE IT'S TOO LATE.

Jilo sprinted towards the swirling flames, the sheer heat of them causing him to perspire instantly, the air so dry that it clogged his throat. He made sure Ka-Del was at the ready and he wasn't afraid to use it to knock the enemies down. Maybe Ka-Del was not a spear made for blood, but he still didn't know what it was capable of, and the last time he'd seen it used, it had been shoved through his father's back.

He collided with a soldier, the impact causing the man to turn around. Scraggly beard whiskers, an ear that had been partially removed at some point, and gnarly teeth painted the man against the harsh light of the fire. The soldier grunted in annoyance, swiftly meeting Jilo's chest with a huge boot and sending him into the forest floor. Jilo grunted as he tasted dirt.

As he lurched upright, the soldier's eyebrows drew together in disbelief, and Jilo rolled over to grab Ka-Del. But the man leapt like a hyo cat, jagged teeth bared, and came crashing down on the spear and Jilo's arm. He felt his wrist crunch and he twisted in pain. It was broken, and his hand became instantly numb. The man held Ka-Del and, getting up from his knees, kept the throbbing blue spearhead at Jilo's throat. The other Theradorans and Scov were nowhere to be seen. This was it. This was the moment he'd die, and his great lineage of Sai-Kathan's leaders would end forevermore.

He gulped, the last of the saliva available to him sliding like tar down his throat as the smoke continued to dry his mouth. The soldier pressed the tip of Ka-Del into Jilo's neck, and he closed his eyes.

*We create our reality, little yam.*

The man hesitated. "La! LA!" Jilo cried. He edged back through the dirt, clawing at the ground with his good hand to get back on his feet. The man lunged for him, but the spear did not reach his skin. Perhaps the spear did not *wish* to hurt Jilo, and he watched as the Theradoran man flailed with it in hand. Then, as the spear missed him again, he turned his back on the flames, the soldier, and any indication of where Scov had gone, and ran.

He ran so fast, the breeze pushed against his broken wrist. He ran so fast, the pads of his feet bled as they were punctured by fallen branches. He ran so fast, he could nearly be convinced that if he stopped, he'd be safe.

Eventually, the terrain of the Greenwood changed and the forest fire was barely a glimmer between the trees. He took a breath and decided on a place to rest. A grand ollg tree stood in the middle of a patch of shrubs, and beneath its canopy, two massive roots created a kind of den for him to sit within. He took his breaths slowly, watching trails of steam exit his lips as the full moon shining overhead cast its dim white glow over the forest. He looked at his wrist, bent entirely the wrong way, and sucked his teeth in pain. Within months, he was back to where he had started, before he'd been found by the Hidden Ones and taken in. He was alone again. It felt like the Sickness had come and gone, except all that raged in the distance now was its opposite: fire.

He reached around to the strap on his back, looking for the comfort he'd found in his father's spear. But Ka-Del was gone, given to the enemy. By him. Why hadn't he done more to stop them from taking it? How would he ever guide himself home to the Nestler's village?

Where was his life to go now? A sad, lonely boy, abandoned by everyone he'd loved, hiding in a vast, mysterious forest.

*To anyone who finds themselves with nobody,* he thought, *I will be there for you. One day. No child will live like this if I can help it. No matter the cost.*

He closed his eyes for a moment, hoping the pain in his arm would fade. Only a moment ... to rest ...

---

When Jilo came to, sweat beaded on his brow so intensely, he thought the dew had gotten to him. He breathed billows of steam and shivered in the dark, cold night. Looking out into the bushes and long grass, he noticed a large rock right by him that he had not seen before. Had anyone been past here?

He wriggled out of the enclosure of roots, studying the rock from afar. As he sidled up to it, his breath caught. The cut of grief would not end with his father.

The elder Zya lay, cold and lifeless with her neck torn open, right beside the tree where he'd hidden. He'd been next to her when they'd killed her, and he hadn't woken up. Bloody paw prints covered the grass and the long, flat fern runners on the ground. How much more death had come to the Hidden Ones on this night, the night of their Great Hunt, because of him? He gritted his teeth, trying not to sob.

They'd wanted Ka-Del, he realised. And they had stopped at nothing to get it. Maybe, now that they had the spear, the pain would stop. The fire would end. Maybe nobody else would die.

"The weasel's dead, Scalmer!" a voice called from nearby. Jilo ducked under the coverage of the shrubs and edged away, back to the ollg tree.

"Good," replied a deeper, more muffled voice. "Burn the body, then. I don't like what these weasels are capable of."

"A dead weasel's a dead weasel," the other chuckled. "We could eat it and keep the skull."

"Just do it!" At that moment, the men came out into the ferny spot where Zya's spent body was. Jilo watched them, making out the familiar mask of the Priest of Dirt. The other Theradoran soldiers were all with him, including, at the back of the pack, the man who held Ka-Del, its blue glimmer still showing through the fabric he had wrapped it up in.

A soldier stepped up to Zya's lifeless frame, torch in hand. He bent down and the fire crackled along the surface of her skin. Jilo steeled himself. *Stop the tears. Stop the pain. Stay alive.*

"Now it's just the boy we need to find," the priest called Scalmer said as the small Nestler body caught alight.

"He ran this direction. I told you," said the one with Ka-Del. "Can this grindel show us the way?"

"Perhaps," the priest said. "Its glow has gotten brighter. Let's keep on, then."

Another group of men entered the space from deeper in the woods, a priest at their helm. Scalmer bent his masked head in greeting. "Reverend," he said. "We found the grindel."

"Ah!" the other priest replied. His skull mask was even cruder than the other ones: a small deer head, it appeared to be. Nails decorated the top of the head, hammered in a random fashion all over its surface. "Well done, Brother. Let us take it back to the capital. The Emperor and that ... woman will be pleased. It seems that menace creature from Piat tipped us off correctly. We'll have to pay him as promised."

"What about the boy?" asked Scalmer.

"Leave the boy." The one in command shrugged. "He'll freeze in these woods before morning comes."

"But sir. He is a southerner. A Kathani boy, here, in the Hidden Forest?"

"It's none of our business who he is, Brother. Our business is the spear. And we've got it now. We've let enough blood run tonight; I wouldn't dare provoke these feral creatures any more than we already have. Pack up your men; we're going home."

Jilo shivered and huddled in the roots of the ollg tree, not daring to venture out. The moon passed over the land as the distant footsteps of the Theradorans faded. Silence proceeded, the kind that cut through one's heart and kept them idly awake.

The Great Hunt was over, the Hidden Ones decimated, and Ka-Del was gone.

# NOW

## *2055 AS*

"The Commander will see you now," a Nestler called Vlac said.

Jilo and Scov had been waiting with Barsh for hours now, sitting in the hot little tent on the edge of the Outfields campsite. Ka-Del was no more, and the pain of its final moments still stung, like a set of sharp claws pulling on Jilo's very soul.

It was the last remnant of his people, and all he'd wanted had been to save it. Reclaim it. Keep the memory of his father, mother, and ancestors alive for as long as possible.

But now, Ka-Del was gone, broken into hundreds of slivers of wood, like a rotten trunk that a child pressed their boots into just to feel it crunch.

He felt tired. Haggard, even. It wasn't a normal kind of exhaustion. It was existential, as though part of him was missing.

The trio stood: Barsh with his confident, eye-patched face; Scov, who leant over in nearly just as tired a manner as Jilo; and Jilo himself, who only wanted this over and done with.

The tent was connected to several other tents via canvas tunnels. In each tent there was an above-ground station and a below-ground section that had been dug and reinforced by Burrower officials. This commander, according to Vlac, was a Nestler, however, and that meant he wouldn't be down in a ditch unless he was thrown into it.

When they reached the final tent, an old but robust Nestler sat before them, tucked in behind a desk, featherquill and ink out on the surface before him. Long whiskers sculpted his grey-coated maw, and the pads of his paws were torn and weathered. Some of the fur along the Nestler's head was in tufts only, patches of baldness showing through in places. The Commander was Garv, a Nestler elder Jilo hadn't seen in many years.

"Please, enter," Commander Garv said. "But not you, Burrower. You may leave."

Barsh winced at the Nestler but complied. "'S been a pleasure, Kathani," he said, outstretching a paw, which Jilo took in a firm grip.

"And you, Burrower. We would not be standing here if it weren't for your help." Jilo could feel Scov frown at him.

"Nestler," Barsh said, nodding at Scov. "Chin up, as they say. You've got this. Be fine." He shook as though he'd been made wet with the discomfort of having to say nice things to a Nestler. "You know what Barsh means. Let's leave it there, then, eh?"

With that, the scraggly Burrower mercenary disappeared, heading back down the tunnel and into the first hole he found.

Silence settled in the room as the old Nestler crossed his paws together on the desktop. "Jilo, son of Hiro. Do you remember me?"

Jilo sighed. "Of course I remember you, Garv."

"Garv is glad." The Commander certainly did not show it. "But Garv is ... sorry to hear of your father's spear. Luminous artifacts are not to be trifled with, and it seems we have learned our lesson."

"Ka-Del had to be destroyed," Jilo said, swallowing. He had no need to mention the sliver he'd kept from the shattered blade. "If it was going to happen, it would be at my hands. Ka-Del was all I had left from my life with the tribe. There are barely any Kathani left in this world now, Garv. I cannot overstate the pain it caused me to see Ka-Del leave this world as well. But with that sacrifice, perhaps we may all live some more to see this war through." He gritted his teeth. He would not feel the other pain. The other loss he had yet to endure. *But Talei was no mother to me.*

"Well ... The war front is worsening by the day, it seems. Victory may no longer favour the alliance." Garv drew up his featherquill and planted a firm dot on a frayed parchment map before him. With his other paw, he gestured at them to come closer.

Jilo took a long look at the map as he approached the old sergeant's desk. It showed the northern part of Q'ara, but it was decimated by red lines, messy and overlapping. Garv's quill marked with a blotch a mass of land between the borders of the Adiran Outfields and the south of Ghabbat.

"The Ghabbatian reinforcements from the north are dwindling," he said. "Therador contests our allied forces in the Outfields, and Adira has fallen back to rebuild. Garv has seen horrors in this war that you could never imagine." He shook his head, morose. "In the past week, a reserve Theradoran force has cut off access to the Adiran border at the Mountain Pass. Aobia and Garv's own people are unable to cross with their current numbers, and so they wait with bated breath for someone to make the first move.

"It is not sensible, Garv thinks, for Therador to split their force across so many fronts, especially with a lack of support from Piat and the Sethi."

Jilo held up a hand. This was not where he was supposed to be, and he knew it. He'd seen it in the many futures Ka-Del had shown him. "Garv, I cannot accept a mission involved so heavily in the conflict. I feel I am called elsewhere." *Away from water, away from ... all this.* But it wasn't just to be away from things. He had work to do.

Garv frowned. "Good earth! Where will you go?"

He'd thought about this every second of every day since Ka-Del had been destroyed, reflecting on his life, his purpose, and everyone he'd lost. He could not let that happen to anyone again. Not on his watch.

"I'll go to Relond. Thousands of refugees flock there from the capital *and* the Empire, people who don't want to observe the war at all. There are so many abandoned, orphaned, or worse. My duty is with those who have nobody. Like the Hidden Ones took me into the Greenwood, I can only try to do the same for those who need someone. Not a parent or mentor ... Just ... someone."

Garv studied him for a second before harrumphing. "Well enough, Cousin. Your nobility exceeds you. Garv hopes you find fulfilment in whatever you choose to do, but know we will miss your aptitude in this war."

Jilo nodded, but he was firm in his decision. "I understand. But there are those who have lost everyone they loved. And there is nobody to take them in, especially not while this fight goes on. It drains our resources and our spirit day after day. What I can give back to those who need it, I will give back."

Garv nodded. "Then you must say your farewells. Scov, you will go to the mountain and fight with Aobia. Garv will be going too, at Cavtil's command."

Jilo gasped as he and the little Nestler looked at one another. He'd practically grown up with Scov. He'd spent all these years by his side since he had been taken into the Greenwood.

"It is only one ending, Cousin," Scov whispered. "Scov will never forget you."

Tears blurred Jilo's vision. "What if you don't come back?"

"Then you have years of history to remember, and Scov will die knowing he had the greatest friend in the world."

"You better come back," Jilo said, gritting his teeth through the sniffles. "You better come to Relond and eat from all the bakeries."

"Scov will do better than that, Cousin." The small creature smirked. "If Scov makes it back, Scov will open his own bakery." Scov grinned as he said the words, a drop of liquid rolling down the fur of his right cheek. He was right, as always. This wasn't the end. Just *an* ending.

"Well," Scov said, turning to Garv. "When do we leave?"

"Dawn."

---

They spent the rest of the night in the Outfields camp, drinking sapwine and reminiscing on times past. The air was thick with memory, and between recalling moments where they had shared life, floated apart, and come together again, they got through a lot of the wine available to them. When enough drink had been savoured and the only bodily response was to lie on one's back, Jilo found himself looking up at the stars next to Scov on a hessian mat.

"I always think of those stars as the ones we've lost," he said quietly. The night was still and warm besides a far-away symphony of crickets.

"You are wise to see loss the way you do, Cousin," Scov murmured in reply. "One more soul to brighten our skies … It is a noble thought."

"I have nothing else," Jilo admitted. "I lost my people, my home, and my parents. But in all the times I've been alone since,

I've found solace in the night sky. It helps with the pain of it all. Maybe Father is up there, maybe not. But what I tell myself shapes my reality. My mother told that to me many times as a child."

"Scov does not know the pain of losing a father, Jilo. But if he is up there, as you say, at least he shines through the darkness now." The Nestler did not speak for a moment, and Jilo pondered the notion that his father could be there, a light in the dark. "What of your mother?" Scov asked eventually.

Jilo sighed. Ka-Del had not predicted a future without his mother. It had predicted a future without itself. "My mother died a long time ago, Scov. I'll leave the past where it belongs. Haven't I lost enough?"

"Loss is difficult, Cousin," Scov began, "but it is within the natural scope of things."

"And yet, it weighs on me that I should use it against itself." Jilo propped himself up on his elbows so he could look at Scov. "I will use whatever is left of my life to improve the lives of the children who have nobody, Scov. This I swear. Where better to do so than in the one city where the east and west converge?"

Scov breathed through his nose. "Scov will stop at nothing to survive this war, Cousin, just so he can see what you accomplish. You can do anything, Jilo. Anything at all."

He stood, brushing bits of grass from his fur. "This is the last time we will see each other until the war is over, Scov fears. Farewell, Cousin Jilo. May the light go with you."

Jilo closed his eyes, unyielding to the moment. It tore at him to leave Scov alone. But Scov was capable and smart, and had been the reason they'd escaped Piat with their lives in the first place.

"May the light go with you, too …" Jilo reached out, gripping the Nestler's paw. "Cousin."

THE END *of*
THE CHILD OF THE GREENWOOD

## Thank you, Fellow Tree-Dweller

Thank you so much for reading *The Child of the Greenwood!* This is not only a darker, more character-driven story for me; it is also an alternative starting point to *The Song of the Sleepers.* So whether you started here, or finished here (for now), I hope you loved every second of it. The tumultuous happenings on Q'ara, however, are not over. To stay up to date with me and my work, please check out my mailing list at:

www.joshuawalkerauthor.com/subscribe

You'll find the companion narrative to this book, *The Rest to the Gods,* over there, too. Both are great entry points to the series.

Nothing fulfils me more than getting my work into the hands of readers. If you wouldn't mind leaving me a review on Goodreads and Amazon, (or if you can't, a star rating would also be fabulous), I can do exactly that. Reviews are like water in the desert, a way for me to keep writing sustainably.

Josh
February 2025

## *Acknowledgements*

As small as these novellas are, they are written to pack a punch, and the background help needed to get them to where they are in your hands now is no small feat.

Firstly, I thank my Creator, for giving me the strength to improve my work with each and every story.

To my family, for consistently supporting my reading habit (could be considered as enabling my addiction, but that's neither here nor there), and cheering me on from the sidelines as I continue to publish: thank you.

To Alice, for being my Number One Ride or Die. As always, I finish a book and then have time to kick back with you and catch up on *The Great British Bake-Off*. Here's to many more years of that. You have all my love.

To my beta team: all of you were exceptional to work with, providing critical insights, plot awareness, and of course, enthusiasm for the story at all the right moments. Without you, this book would have never been ready for the next step in the process. Thank you to Carina, Isaac, Justin, Kris, Kenneth, Vivian, Nicholas, Ben and Amina.

To the Break-Ins, you are all my MVP's. Scott Palmer, Rob Leigh, Isaac Hill, Kaden Love, Adrian M Gibson, Louise Holland, Calum Lott, Jonathan Weiss, Sam Paisley, Bryan Wilson, Francisca Liliana, Andrew Watson, ZS Diamanti, Nicholas W Fuller, and Aaron M Payne—as we go into Year 2, I'm as excited as ever to do it with you all.

To my double whammy editing team: Sarah, your awareness of line impact is incomparable. You've really made this novella shine. Isabelle, your proofreading is incredible as always, and provides me with the cleanest final files. Thank you both.

To my cover artist Stef: I told you when we worked together the first time that there was something special about the cover for *The Rest to the Gods*. This one, however, is a game changer. And I can't wait to work with you again on Novella #3! The same goes for my wonderful cartographer Josh Hoskins, who captured the continent of Q'ara perfectly. You're both legendary.

To the community of readers and writers online who have supported me: I can't possibly recall all of you, but particular shout-outs are owed to the following: Kristen Shafer, Boe Kelley, Bob from BlueSmokeFire and the entirety of the SFF Insiders team; Kris the Fictional Escapist; Livia J Elliot; SK Putt; Ainy Cormac; Luke Schulz; Brenden Pugh from Writing Quest; Carina (@carina_inkdrinker); Graham Blades (@thewulverslibrary); Katee Stein; RJ Lavender; Kayla from Kay's Hidden Shelf; Esmay Rosalyne; Matt from Beard of Darkness; Ari Augustine; Amanda (@fulltimebookish); Anie (@meetmeinmalkovich); Abel Montero; Ben Leyland; Armilia (@armilia.bookdiary); and SO many more.

Lastly, to you, dear reader. Without you, the Luminous World would remain in my mind alone. For as long as you are here to listen, I'll be here to tell stories.

# ABOUT THE AUTHOR

Joshua Walker is a fantasy author currently living in Sydney, Australia. He works as a primary school English teacher, and likes to read, brew beer, and hang out with his wife and BFD (Big Fluffy Dog) in his free time.

To find out more about The Song of the Sleepers series, head to www.joshuawalkerauthor.com.

www.ingramcontent.com/pod-product-compliance
Lightning Source LLC
LaVergne TN
LVHW031310310125
802554LV00027B/910